"What's wron

Chase frowned in the rearview mirror.

Diana looked behind her, but the shooters' car was gone. "Where'd they go?"

"They just took off in the opposite direction."

She glanced at the child next to her, then faced him in the mirror. "Why doesn't that comfort me as much as it should?"

"I don't know...but I feel the same way."

Finally, something the two of them could agree on. A low rumble vibrated through the car as a section of stone suddenly gave way, crashing down the side of the mountain.

"Hold on to her!" Chase called.

Diana barely registered the rockslide before a giant boulder slammed into the driver's side of the car. She flung her body across Emmie, gripping the back seat on either side of the little girl to brace her.

Another loud crash, followed by squealing tires, as Chase struggled to regain control, then lost his battle. The car tipped precariously over the edge, teetering over the ravine plunging down the mountainside. Even as Diana closed her eyes and prayed, the next barrage sent them over the edge.

Deena Alexander grew up in a small town on eastern Long Island where she lived up until a few years ago and then relocated to Clermont, Florida, with her husband, three children, son-in-law and four dogs. Now she enjoys long walks in nature all year long, despite the occasional alligator or snake she sometimes encounters. Her love for writing developed after the birth of her youngest son, who had trouble sleeping through the night.

Books by Deena Alexander

Love Inspired Suspense

Crime Scene Connection
Shielding the Tiny Target
Kidnapped in the Woods
Christmas in the Crosshairs
Hunted for the Holidays
Hiding the Witness

Visit the Author Profile page at LoveInspired.com.

HIDING THE WITNESS

DEENA ALEXANDER

LOVE INSPIRED SUSPENSE
INSPIRATIONAL ROMANCE

LOVE INSPIRED® SUSPENSE
INSPIRATIONAL ROMANCE

ISBN-13: 978-1-335-98045-8

Hiding the Witness

Love Inspired
22 Adelaide St. West, 41st Floor
Toronto, Ontario M5H 4E3, Canada
www.LoveInspired.com

Printed in Lithuania

MIX
Paper | Supporting
responsible forestry
FSC® C021394

Yea, though I walk through the valley of the shadow of death, I will fear no evil: for thou art with me; thy rod and thy staff they comfort me.
—*Psalms* 23:4

This book is lovingly dedicated to
Greg, Elaina, Steve, Nicky and Logan—
you are my greatest blessings.

ONE

Diana Cameron knew better than to drive while exhausted, especially on the winding mountain road that led to the isolated log cabin she called home. But tonight, she was doing it, anyway. She cracked the window, filling the Jeep with the scent of crisp autumn air, fallen leaves and the coming storm. The scenery—an entire mountain speckled with the vibrant orange, red and gold hues of fall—would have kept her awake if it wasn't three o'clock in the morning and pitch-black. Even the moonlight couldn't force its way through the thick cloud cover that heralded the coming storm—which was one of the reasons she'd decided to head home rather than stay at the firehouse when her shift had ended. That, and the indescribable urge nudging her home, a voice she'd learned a long time ago to heed.

Plus, the last thing she wanted was to stay at the firehouse and have to explain to her fellow firefighters the screams that so often preceded her waking. She needed a good night's sleep in her own bed. Hopefully, without the nightmares that so often plagued her, though she doubted that would be the case.

Home. Even after four years living in the mountains of upstate New York, as far as she could get from the mild climate and palm trees she'd grown up with in Central Florida, it still sometimes felt surreal to call the area home. When she'd fled Orlando four years ago, after the one man she should have been able to trust had betrayed her, she'd harbored doubts she'd ever be able to find somewhere to call home again. She'd never expected the sense of camaraderie and kinship she'd found at the Shady Creek Fire Department.

She shifted, uncomfortable with, but not surprised at, the direction her thoughts had wandered. Memories often crept in during the darkest hours, when exhaustion left her vulnerable, when she didn't have the strength to battle the pain, the betrayal, the heartache, the fear. Liam Barlow had been her fiancé, her hero, her everything. Her perfect match—or so she'd thought. How could she have made such a terrible mistake? How had she missed the signs, when she'd been trained to see them, had volunteered to work with abused women at the local shelter?

Was that what had driven her to help people? To protect those who were in danger? To become a firefighter, as Liam had been, to atone for his sins committed in her name? Did it still drive her to do more? Would it ever be enough?

No. Probably not.

Not when she'd failed to recognize her own reflection mirrored in the dead eyes of the women she'd tried to help, before her fian— No. She refused to think of him in that way anymore. He was the criminal who would spend the rest of his life in prison for burning down that women's shelter. Not that a lifetime of incarceration could pay for all the lives he stole that day in a fit of selfish rage.

Tears shimmered in her eyes, blurring the already dangerous road. Diana swiped the tears from her cheeks. They were not for Liam—she'd never shed a single tear for him, nor would she—but for all the people he'd killed just to take something she loved away from her, something that stole her attention from him, that took her from his side when he wanted her there to lift him up, to help him attain his goals.

Well, at least she could rest comfortably knowing he'd spend the rest of his life locked behind bars, where he couldn't hurt anyone else. Unless you counted the thoughts of him that taunted her every time she hovered near sleep.

Lightning sizzled across the clouds then struck too close, raising goose bumps. A massive peal of thunder followed on its heels. At this rate, she'd count her blessings if she could get even a few hours of sleep, just enough so it wouldn't feel like sandpaper scraping over her eyes every time she blinked tomorrow. Drier-than-usual conditions, a mountain full of fallen leaves and brush and a lightning storm—talk about a recipe for disaster.

Gravel crunched beneath her tires as her eyelids fluttered and she veered onto the nearly nonexistent shoulder separating the road from the ravine. She jerked straighter in the seat and eased off the gas pedal. Better to take a few extra minutes and arrive safely. Hadn't she responded to enough accidents where drivers had fallen asleep at the wheel? She eyed the twelve-hour-old half-empty coffee cup in the cup holder and sighed as she reached for it. Cold, disgusting caffeine was still caffeine. It was better than nothing. She only had ten minutes left to drive. At this point, she'd make it home quicker than she could return to the firehouse and—

A massive explosion rocked the night. She jumped, startled, the gigantic ball of light a few yards up the mountain momentarily blinding her. She jerked the wheel to the right, spilled the coffee everywhere, slammed into a tree—better than plunging into the ravine—and struggled to brace herself as the airbag exploded. Her ears rang as she disentangled herself from the airbag and took a quick inventory. Other than the ringing in her ears, everything seemed to be in working order. Of course, that could be shock. Either way...

Without bothering to wipe the coffee off herself, she tumbled out of the Jeep and whipped her cell phone out of her pocket, dialing as she ran toward the fire visible not far ahead.

Wait! Catching herself, she ran back to the Jeep and grabbed the fire extinguisher from its holder in the back. She needed to clear her head. Since she had no idea what had exploded, she had to move fast in case there were victims. Plus, with the current conditions, the entire mountain could go up in flames if they didn't get control quickly.

"Nine-one-one. What is your emergency?"

Setting a course on the straightest route to the orange glow of flames, Diana began weaving between trees. She used two fingers and her elbows against trunks and branches to pull herself up steeper points, and scrambled over rocks and boulders while clutching the fire extinguisher in one hand and pressing the phone against her ear with the other as she relayed the situation and her position. Thankfully, the call went quickly, and when it was done, she stuffed her phone back into her pocket. With one hand free, she moved faster, the dead leaves crunching beneath her feet a constant reminder of the immense amount of fuel available to feed the flames.

And it would take time for rescue workers to reach her, leaving all the area's residents in danger. Rental properties dotted the mountain, which was a popular tourist destination this time of year. She could only pray whatever had exploded had been empty. The scent of smoke prodded her to pick up the pace.

When she reached a clearing surrounding a log hunting lodge and spotted an SUV in the driveway, her heart sank. She barely resisted the urge to run straight through the front door, which was open—from the force of the explosion, or had someone escaped? She had no idea, and should wait for backup, but there wasn't time.

With each second ticking by like a cannon blast in her head, Diana set down the fire extinguisher and yanked her long hair into a tight bun against her head, then tied it with a scrunchie from her wrist. She whipped off her loose-fitting windbreaker—dangling fabric could be a hazard in a fire situation—and dropped it on the ground, leaving her in T-shirt, jeans and her favorite olive-green work boots. She began assessing the situation—flames engulfed the entire back and one side of the cabin. She scanned the clearing for survivors who might be unable to call out. Finding none, she grabbed the fire extinguisher and propelled herself across the brittle patch of brown grass, up three steps to the front porch and through the doorway. The first thing to hit her was the smell of gasoline. Between that and the intensity of the fire, she had no doubt an accelerant had been used, that the fire had been intentionally set. She filed away that information for later. Right now...

Flames licked up the living room walls, devouring the curtains on the back French doors directly across from her, then ravenously searched for more. She held on to the fire extinguisher. No way would she be able to suppress these flames on her own. The cabin was going to be a loss.

Thick smoke stung her eyes. Tendrils burned their way

down the back of her throat. Tears impeded her vision. She had to check for victims and get out of there. "Hello? I'm with the Shady Creek Fire Department. Is anyone here?"

She almost stumbled over the first victim. A man. Mid-thirties, wearing jeans, a denim jacket and work boots. Had he already been dressed? Or had he thrown on clothes when the fire started? She crouched beside him, felt for a pulse—nothing—and noticed the wound on his head. She was too late, but it wasn't the flames or the smoke that had gotten him. She was certain she was staring at a bullet wound. He'd been executed, if she wasn't mistaken.

Fear gripped her throat, threatening to squeeze it closed. Or maybe that was the smoke. She felt along the floor, moving toward the sidewall, dragging the fire extinguisher with her. Smoke billowed overhead. But now, she had a new problem. It would be bad enough if an arsonist lurked nearby. If the criminal was still around, did that mean a killer could be watching her? If someone had gone to the trouble of firebombing the cabin to cover their tracks, surely they'd have waited around to make sure the flames did their job. And if they'd seen her run into the cabin—

Her hand brushed fabric, and she found a woman, also fully dressed, with a matching bullet wound. Diana yanked out her cell phone and aimed the flashlight at the woman, committing as many details as possible to memory. She felt for a pulse, even knowing she was too late to save either of them, and made note of the ivy tattoo running from behind her left ear, down her neck and disappearing into her collar. Hopefully, it would help the investigators ID the victim. It was time to move. She had to get out of there. She tucked the cell phone back in her pocket, crouched beside the woman and slid her hands into place beneath her arms.

She might not be able to save their lives, but she'd at least get one of them out of there and perhaps preserve any evi—

A soft sob sounded from nearby.

Abandoning any hope of preserving evidence, along with the fire extinguisher, Diana whirled toward the sound. Seeing nothing, she inched forward on her hands and knees, feeling her way toward the corner of the room. When she reached the wall, she pressed a hand against it and used it to guide her toward the corner. Between the smoke and the tears, visibility was practically nil.

Then she spotted a small bundle curled in the corner of the room behind an armchair. She scrambled the last few feet across the floor, a coughing fit racking her body. Her chest ached as she reached out and turned the child over, resisting the urge to close her eyes as she prayed the child hadn't also been shot. The pressure on her chest increased as she dragged the child into her arms, lifted her and ran, bent at the waist, for the doorway.

The second explosion lifted her off her feet just as she cleared the front porch, flinging her across the clearing as she desperately clung to the child. She landed hard on her left hip. Her shoulder wrenched—probably dislocated—as she twisted to take the brunt of the impact, and hit a tree trunk hard. Her neck snapped backward, and the world did one long, slow roll.

Fighting dizziness, she lay the little girl on the cold ground and felt for a pulse. There, but weak. It took a moment to recognize the *pop, pop, pop* of gunfire. Something ricocheted from a tree, stung her cheek. Ignoring the pain, she covered the child with her body, then rolled them both into the brush.

"Diana!"

Oh, thank You, God.

"Naomi?" Naomi Adams, Shady Creek's sheriff, was a good friend of Diana's. Her throat burned, but she needed to warn her. "Sniper! Get down!"

Naomi's eyes widened as she went instantly on alert.

More shots rang out, pelting the trees and brush.

Diana hunched over the little girl, keeping as low as possible, desperate to assess her condition, but unable to do so under the barrage of automatic-weapon fire.

"Stay down!" Naomi crouched in front of them and returned fire. "You hit?"

"No." Was she? She remembered the sting on her cheek, but it was more likely tree bark that had hit her. Her probably dislocated shoulder screamed and begged her to keep still, but that would keep for now. "No. I think I'm okay, but I have an unconscious child who needs medical attention."

The gunshots stopped, and Naomi called for backup— all two Shady Creek deputies, one of whom she'd be dragging out of bed.

Taking advantage of the reprieve, Diana straightened enough to check the little girl's pulse and search for any life-threatening injuries.

"Hey." A delicate but strong hand rested on her uninjured shoulder. Naomi fell to her knees in front of her and inspected her cheek. "You sure you're okay?"

Diana nodded, examining the child for injuries, feeling along her extremities.

Accepting her word, the sheriff got straight to business. "What do you need?"

"Oxygen," she croaked out, her voice raspy from the smoke.

Naomi stood, her jeans and fleece-lined flannel, instead

of her uniform, a good indication she'd been home when the call had come in. She pulled her cell phone from her pocket.

"Two dead inside. Gunshot wounds to the head. Execution style." Diana relayed the information calmly, professionally, despite the churning in her gut at the memory.

"You're sure?" But the sheriff's eyes had already gone hard as she scanned the immediate area for any further threat.

Diana nodded, sucking in deep, greedy gulps of the cool night air. Thankfully, the wind blew the smoke away from them. She half listened to the sheriff issue orders into the phone as she studied the little girl.

She couldn't be more than two or three years old. Shoulder-length brown hair had been pulled into pigtails, one of which had come loose. Her breathing was shallow, becoming more erratic. Her eyes squeezed tighter, crinkling the corners. Not unconscious, but pretending?

Diana smoothed the hair back from her delicate features as gently as possible. When she started to speak, only a raspy whisper emerged, and she coughed before trying again. "It's okay, sweetie. You can open your eyes. You're safe now. I'm a firefighter with the Shady Creek Fire Department."

Tears leaked from the corners of the little girl's eyes and streamed down her cheeks, then she sucked in a breath and sobbed.

"Shh... Baby, it's okay. You're safe." What had this child witnessed? It wasn't bad enough the cabin she was in had just exploded and gone up in flames, but were the two victims inside her parents? Had she witnessed them being shot? "My name is Diana, and I'm going to keep you safe. I promise. Can you tell me if you're hurt?"

She slitted her eyes open and studied Diana for a moment as if searching for the truth in her words. Her eyes were bloodshot, the pupils dilated. Effect from the smoke? Or had she hit her head?

Diana remained perfectly still, cradling her arm against her and fighting the eddy of blackness encroaching in her peripheral vision, careful not to move suddenly and startle the frightened child.

Naomi leaned over her shoulder from behind and whispered into her ear. "We're organizing a search team, and the fire department is almost here. Do you know if anyone else was inside?"

"I don't know," she admitted. There hadn't been time to check for more survivors. She'd barely had time to get out with the little girl. She crammed the guilt into a small box in her mind, where it would have plenty of company, and closed it off to examine later.

Naomi's voice lowered even further. "Do you know if she saw anything?"

The little girl met Diana's gaze for an instant, the fear in her eyes contagious, then her eyes fluttered closed and she rolled onto her side and started to cough.

"I don't know that, either."

"Okay." Naomi patted Diana's uninjured shoulder. "All right. The paramedics are just pulling in. And you are going to the hospital."

"I—"

"Don't even bother to argue." She held up a hand, the no-nonsense determination in her expression a stark contrast to her petite stature. "It's an order."

One Diana couldn't really argue against, as she lost her battle for consciousness and toppled to the side.

* * *

The last thing Chase Mitchell needed was a kid to look after. All he'd wanted was a peaceful week off to spend with his sister after a particularly difficult case with Jameson Investigations, where he worked as a private security agent. Was that too much to ask? Apparently so, since his second day in Shady Creek had him rushing to the hospital at Naomi's frantic call. And Naomi wasn't prone to panic. If she was seeking his help, it was because things had spiraled out of control.

But a child to protect? She, of all people, should have known better than to ask that of him. She'd learned the hard way she'd be better off recruiting anyone else. And yet, now, here he was.

But only because Shady Creek's Sheriff's Department consisted of his sister and two deputies and was not capable of providing protective custody and conducting an investigation at the same time. Not without help. Still, if anyone but Naomi, who'd suffered her own share of tragedies, had asked, he'd have said no. Children were way out of Chase's area of expertise. Not that he didn't like kids— he did. But after an FBI assignment to protect a child had ended in him losing both his wife, who'd been his partner on the case, and the child, Chase steered clear—of children, of relationships, of attachments. Naomi was his only exception, even though he'd failed her. He had no idea why she even still spoke to him. And look where hanging on to that relationship had just landed him—about as far outside of his comfort zone as he could get.

Chase exited the elevator on the second floor, strode through the double doors into the chaos of the ward and sighed. He wasn't really being fair. And he knew that. In his head, at least. Naomi never would have asked him for help if she wasn't in desperate need of a bodyguard to protect a child who may or may not have witnessed two adults, possibly her parents, being brutally murdered.

Naomi, a petite sturdy woman with a cap of blond frizz and muddy brown eyes, hurried toward him and held out her arms. "Chase, thank you for coming."

He frowned but pulled her into his arms for a quick hug. "Of course, I came, Naomi. But you knew I would."

She smiled, bringing a sparkle to those brown eyes. "Still, thank you."

"Sure." He scanned the hallway. With no idea what threat might exist, he tried to keep watch everywhere at once.

"Oh, and you might want to do something about that rock-hard expression of yours." She winked and gestured to a pair of double doors. "Otherwise, someone might mistake you for the killer."

A smile tugged at him. Unsure what to say, he started in the direction she'd indicated, then fell into step at her side when she turned and started down the corridor at a brisk pace. "You didn't say much when you called, just that the child was found in a burning building along with two deceased adults. Have you learned anything further about their identities?"

"One of my officers recovered an ID in the vehicle found in front of the cabin. I'm on my way to show it to Diana now."

"Diana?"

"Diana Cameron. An off-duty firefighter who was first on scene. Since she's the only one who actually saw the victims before the building exploded, I'm hoping she can at least confirm if the male victim she saw was the same man as the photo on the driver's license." She stopped in front of a closed door with the window covered and a deputy standing guard outside. Placing a hand on the door handle, she paused and turned to meet his eyes. "And, um, for the record..."

He studied her, lifted an eyebrow and waited for her to continue.

"You may want to do something to soften that expression *before* you go inside. The child is young, only around two or three years old, and is already traumatized. I don't want her any more frightened than she already is."

He bit back any sarcastic retort and ignored the urge to tell her he didn't deal with children. Instead, he struggled to relax his features.

"I guess that'll have to do for now, but..." She laughed and shook her head, then shoved the door open. "You might wanna keep working on that."

Chase looked up and down the corridor before stepping into the room.

A small child was lying on the gurney, her brown hair spilling around her on the pillow, making her appear even more fragile, and his heart stuttered. How was he supposed to do this? He couldn't. He'd see her safe for the moment, for his sister's sake, because he knew how important it was to her to make sure no one could get to the child, but if Naomi didn't get reinforcements from the state or the FBI quickly, he'd beg Zac Jameson to send another agent as soon as possible.

A woman lifted her head, brushed back a mass of limp auburn waves and regarded him from an armchair beside the little girl's bed. After she gave him the once-over, she pushed to her feet. She narrowed eyes the rich, deep color of dark chocolate at him. "Naomi?"

"This is my brother, Chase Mitchell," the sheriff said with a sigh, as if braced for an argument that had already played out more than once. "He's here to protect you and the little girl until we know more about what's going on."

Wait. What? No one had said anything about protecting a woman, just the child. Although…if the woman was with them, she could care for the little girl, and he could concentrate on security. A win-win, really.

"I already told you, I don't need a bodyguard." She folded one arm across her chest, cradling the other that hung in a sling close to her body, and lifted her chin. The look in her eyes belied her slight stature. And Naomi was complaining about him? Talk about harsh expressions.

Naomi approached her, put a hand on her shoulder and looked her in the eye. "Please, Diana. As your friend, I'm asking you. Please, just go along with this. At least until we know something more. The child wasn't the only witness, you know. And the killer already took shots at you. As soon as we can determine if you are a target, we can reassess the situation. Right now, all I'm asking is for you to hang around here with Chase and the little girl until we figure out what's going on. Besides, if she wakes, it would be good for her to see a familiar face rather than that mug." She waved a hand toward her brother.

Diana's shoulder slumped, and she ran her free hand over the child's hair, smoothing it back so gently from her face the little girl didn't respond. "Fine. For now. But only because I don't want to leave her."

"Thank you."

Diana nodded, and her expression softened. "I'm not trying to be difficult, Naomi. You know that. But I do have to get back to work soon. Last I heard, the fire had begun to spread."

Naomi was already nodding as she pulled a plastic evidence bag from her pocket and held it out to Diana. "But there's nothing you can do with your arm injured, anyway, so just help me out here. Do you recognize this man?"

"As soon as my shoulder feels well enough, I'm going back. Thankfully, it wasn't dislocated." Diana held her gaze for another moment, then took the driver's license from Naomi. She brought the image closer to her face, then quirked her lips and shook her head. "I can't be sure. It was smoky, and my eyes were tearing, and I only checked long enough to be sure he couldn't be helped before moving on, but…I think it's the same man."

Naomi gripped her hand as she took the evidence bag back from her. "Sit down, please."

Diana sighed but did as Naomi asked, returning to her seat at the little girl's side.

Naomi pulled a chair from the corner to sit beside her.

From the comforting gestures and the look of concern as she eyed Diana, Chase had no doubt the two were friends, probably close friends. He hoped that was the case, hoped Naomi had found a way to move past her pain and open her heart to love again.

"I need to go over a few things with you, if you feel up to it now," Naomi said.

"Yeah." Diana nodded, her gaze fixed on the child. "Of course, sure."

Naomi pulled out a notepad and pen. "For now, we'll figure the male victim is the man in the ID photo, but what can you tell me about the woman? Height, weight, age, hair color, any identifying marks?"

Chase folded his arms and stood beside the door. He should probably step outside and monitor the hallway, but the more he understood about the case, the more he'd be able to anticipate what to expect. Hearing it straight from Diana would not only save time, but would also give him a firsthand account rather than reading from a report.

"Um. She had dark hair, kind of long. Slim build. I can't give you a height." Diana frowned, clearly reliving the scene as it played out in her mind. "Wait. The tattoo."

Naomi's gaze shot to Diana, who had pain etched into her features. "Tattoo?"

Chase stepped forward. "What?"

Naomi held up a hand to halt him. "Tell me."

"An ivy tattoo." Diana placed a finger beside her ear, then drew it along a path and explained, "It ran from behind her left ear, down her neck and into her collar."

"Ah, man." Naomi sat back in the chair and massaged the bridge of her nose between a thumb and forefinger, a sign of agitation all too familiar to Chase.

"You knew her?" he asked, though he already knew the answer.

"Sort of." She looked up at him, tears shimmering in her eyes, tears he knew full well she'd never shed. "She showed up outside the station early yesterday morning, caught me on my way inside. She was nervous, jumpy, said she was afraid of her husband and scared for her child. She told me they'd fled New York City because her husband had gotten involved in something illegal with some very shady characters. She was afraid he'd follow her here to Shady Creek. She refused to come inside the station but agreed to meet with me at one of the scenic overlooks—alone—last night.

She never showed, which was why I was in the area and able to make it to you so quickly when the cabin exploded."

She shook her head, frowned, then continued. "If her behavior was any indication, she was terrified of her husband. I got the impression that he was the biggest threat to her safety. That's why I didn't think of her when Diana said a couple was murdered. But those shady characters she mentioned...maybe he had ties to organized crime, or perhaps a gang affiliation—and the people he was aligned with turned on him, killing her, too, to keep her from being a witness. But, of course, that's just a theory for now. We'll need more evidence before we can reach any conclusions."

Chase ran through the scenario in his head, but Naomi was right—they'd need more information before they could come up with answers. Right now, his concern was for his sister, who would no doubt shoulder more than her fair share of guilt that she may have failed the woman and her child. No way could he lose this kid on her. Not again.

"I'm sorry. I—" A coughing fit overtook Diana. She held up a finger for Naomi to wait, rode it out, then cleared her throat and lifted a cup from the tray beside her and sipped. "I should have thought to tell you about the tattoo sooner."

"Hey, don't worry about it." Naomi took the cup from her and set it back on the tray, then bent and hugged Diana. "You were in a car accident, ran into a burning building, were thrown from that building by an explosion, got shot at and lost consciousness. You can be forgiven for not remembering every detail. I'm just glad it came back to you."

She nodded, seeming less than convinced.

Naomi squeezed her shoulder before stepping away. "Thank you, Diana."

"Sure thing." Diana's smile transformed her features,

despite the fact that her face still bore a few spots of soot, along with several scrapes and bruises, and a bandage on her left temple. "Now, go find whoever did this. And be quick about it."

"You're in that much of a hurry to ditch my protection?" Chase asked, curious about the woman who seemed to change expressions at the drop of a hat despite the dire situation.

"No." She turned her gaze on him. "I'm in that much of a hurry to find this little girl's family so she won't have to be so afraid."

Naomi glanced back and forth between them, then laughed out loud, shot them a two-finger salute and muttered, "You two deserve each other," as she walked out of the room.

"So…" Diana's gaze slid over him, as if she was assessing every one of his deepest, darkest secrets with just one look. "Now what?"

He walked the perimeter of the room, opened the door and glanced up and down the corridor, then closed it and moved over to check out the second-floor window that overlooked the roof of the first-story emergency room. "We're going to have to take her to a safe house."

She frowned. "Why would you move her? She's still receiving medical care. They haven't even received all the test results yet."

"Because it's not safe here. We can't protect her amid all the people coming in and out of the hospital. Plus—" he gestured to the four-story building directly across the parking lot "—it would be easy enough for a sniper to set up over there and have a perfect line of sight into her window."

Diana's mouth fell open and hung there for a second

before she snapped it closed. "Are you serious right now? She's a baby. You really think someone would go to such great lengths to… What? Eliminate her?"

He shrugged, reevaluating the whole let-her-take-care-of-the-child train of thought. If she was going to argue with him every step of the way, this was not going to work. And he was not about to explain himself to her every time he made a decision. "We have no idea what we're up against, only that two people have already been shot and killed, and the building they were in—the building someone left that child inside—was firebombed. And then, someone tried to gun down not only both you and the kid, but my sister, too."

Diana swallowed hard and nodded. She looked around the room, slid her gaze up and down the IV pole and the various monitors, then finally settled on the child, seeming less than convinced his suggestion was the right course of action. "Point made, but I'm still not comfortable moving her."

He was saved from arguing further by chaos from outside the room. He opened the door and peered out. He could hear the sounds of people running, screaming, the clatter of a cart upending as someone plowed into it in their haste to flee something. Whatever it was, he wasn't waiting around to find out. At least now she couldn't argue with him about the necessity of moving the little girl. He yanked the fire alarm, then slammed the door closed and whirled straight into Diana.

"Is there a fire?"

"No. I'm not sure what's going on out there, but it's not good."

Her eyes went wide. "Did you just seriously pull the fire alarm when there was no fire?"

He gripped her arms, his hold gentle but firm. "Listen to me. We have to move. Now. I don't know what's happening out there, but whatever it is, people are pretty much trampling each other to get away from it. They need help, and I can't go offer it *and* protect this child. The fire alarm seemed the quickest way to summon backup."

She closed her eyes, inhaled deeply and nodded. "Okay. Alright."

He sidestepped her, disconnected the IV and ripped off the other leads. Even if the girl was awake and cooperative—which they couldn't guarantee—there was no way the child could walk as quickly on her own as they needed her to. Besides, she'd hardly be comfortable walking the cold hospital floor in bare feet. He gestured toward the child, then Diana's injured arm. "Can you carry her?"

If she couldn't, he'd have to, which would leave him unable to use his weapon if needed.

She slid her arm free of the sling. "I'll manage. Just get her in my arms."

He lifted the little girl, cradled her for one flicker of an instant, resisting the urge to promise her he'd keep her safe when he knew full well he might not be able to keep that promise. Then he handed her off to Diana.

To her credit, she winced in pain but said nothing as she sought a comfortable position.

"You sure you're okay?"

"I'm fine. Go." She turned toward the door, but he stopped her with a hand on her arm and pointed toward the window.

The little girl's head popped up, her eyes wide with terror. She clawed at Diana, struggling to free herself.

Diana whispered urgently to her. Whatever she said must have worked, because while the fear remained in the child's expression, she stopped struggling and didn't cry out. Instead, she wrapped her arms and legs around Diana and clung tight.

Screams beat at him from the hallway, prodding him to move.

He had no time to alleviate the child's fears, and even if he could, anything he said to her might well be a lie. He couldn't guarantee her safety—he could only do his best to ensure it. Since there seemed to be no way to open the window, he grabbed the chair Diana had been sitting in, lifted it and smashed the window, then cleared the glass as best he could. "Go. Now."

The child buried her head against Diana.

Diana looked at him like he'd lost his mind, but she didn't argue, and she didn't hesitate, diving through the window onto the roof of the emergency room with the child clutched against her like a pro. Just as he climbed on the sill to follow, the door crashed open and two gunmen opened fire.

TWO

Chase jumped out the window and rolled, then sprung to his feet with a pistol in each hand in one smooth motion—he was surprisingly fast and agile for a man who topped six feet by at least three or four inches, and probably weighed in at a solidly built 210 pounds. "Go! Run! Find cover!"

Were those gunshots following them? Diana was not waiting around to find out. Tucking the little girl against her, Diana ignored the pain screaming through her shoulder and ran. When she reached a large metal storage box, she dropped behind it and searched for a way to get to the ground...and hopefully to safety.

She checked the little girl, who was groggy, terrified, most likely in shock, but she seemed to be holding on even though tremors tore violently through her. "It'll be okay, honey. We'll get you somewhere safe."

The girl said nothing, just popped her thumb in her mouth, closed her eyes and lowered her head against Diana's shoulder.

Chase fired off a shot, then ducked beside her. "We can't stay here."

"There's an emergency ladder in the corner," she pointed

out, but they'd have to cover at least forty feet of open space to reach it.

He dropped his head back, and she could practically see the gears turning as he thought of and dismissed plan after plan…exactly like she was doing. Then he swung his head to the side. The instant he peered around the edge, one of the gunmen fired. Chase got off another shot then yanked himself back.

The gunmen must have taken cover as well, since the pounding of footsteps had stopped. It seemed they were at a bit of an impasse, not that it was likely to last long. They had to get out of there without any of them or any innocent bystanders getting shot. Unfortunately, there was no easy exit.

She scanned the roof, searching for another way off, when something occurred to her. "God, please let me be able to do this without dropping her."

The child clung tighter.

Chase pinned her with the most piercing blue eyes she'd ever seen. "If you want to get off this roof alive, you might want to do less praying and more thinking."

She bristled. "And you might want to do more praying, because that may be the only thing that gets us off this roof alive."

The emergency room entrance should be ten feet ahead… and straight down. Diana hoped she was judging correctly, because she wouldn't have time to look over before jumping. With the box at their back to provide some cover, if she stayed low and caught the gunman by surprise, she might just make it before he could see her, aim and shoot. She pointed toward the roof's edge. "Straight ahead."

Bullets struck the metal box. Seemed their pursuers were growing impatient.

Chase returned fire, then looked in the direction she'd indicated. "What?"

She shifted the little girl's weight and gripped her more firmly, wrapping her arms tightly around her and cradling her head against her so it wouldn't snap back when she jumped. Landing would be unpleasant, to say the least, but they had no other choice. "You're going to have to trust me."

"Honey…" He grinned—*grinned*—which deepened a dimple in his right cheek beneath his closely cropped beard. If not for the fact that she was clutching a child and running from at least two gunmen, she might have decked him right then and there for seeming so amused by this whole thing. What did he think this was? Some kind of deadly game? "I haven't trusted anyone in a very long time."

She shrugged, feigning a nonchalance she didn't feel. "Then just cover me, and you can figure out how to get yourself out of here once I'm gone."

With that, she bent low, protecting the child as best she could, and sprinted for the roof's edge. Gunshots erupted behind her, but she ignored them. She didn't trust the handsome, bitter stranger to protect them, but she could—and did—trust that her prayer had been heard. If God chose to use a smirking jerk to answer it, then she could live with that.

When she reached the low wall surrounding the roof, she clutched the child in an iron grip, prayed she wouldn't miss and vaulted over the wall. The jolt when she landed on the ground sent a wave of pain crashing through her. It squeezed her lungs, robbed her of breath. Her vision turned fuzzy at the edges. No way could she pass out. It would be a death sentence not just for her, but for the little girl and probably Mr. Personality as well.

A loud thump beside her, as Chase landed, forced away some of the haze. "You alright?"

She sucked in a breath, wheezed and choked out, "Yeah."

Without waiting for him to say anything else, she scrambled to her feet. To his credit, he stayed right behind her, providing cover as they retreated. She crossed the walkway, barely looked for oncoming traffic as she ran across the narrow drive that allowed for drop-offs and pick-ups, then hesitated when she remembered she'd been brought in by ambulance and didn't have her car.

"Go right!"

Another barrage of gunfire propelled her in the direction he'd ordered. Weaving between the parked cars to keep some kind of cover between her and the gunmen, she ran. Even though the child was tiny, and Diana was trained to carry a grown man down a ladder, carrying her while running with her injured shoulder was beginning to take its toll. Even the adrenaline rush wouldn't push her much farther. She was going to have to rest. She hugged the little girl tighter and dug deep into her depleted energy reserves. She'd already been exhausted even before this ordeal had started, but she could find the strength for this. She had to.

"Right there." The lights blinked on a black SUV with tinted windows. Unfortunately, the chirps also probably alerted their pursuers to their position. No matter. Nothing they could do about it now.

She flung the back door open and stared at the empty back seat. "There's no car seat for her."

Chase put one hand on the door and the other on the back

window, caging her between him and the seat. "You want to follow the rules, or do you want to survive?"

She wanted to snap back at him, but she clamped down on the urge. What was it about him that had her so riled up? It's not like she was a stickler for the rules. After all, she had run into that burning building to see if anyone needed help, despite knowing she should wait for backup. But for some reason, he sure pushed her buttons. She swallowed hard and reminded herself that he was literally standing between her and danger. "I just want to keep this child safe."

Though his blond-streaked brown hair was short in the back and on the sides, the top was longer and ruffled when he blew up an exasperated breath. Under other circumstances, the thought of his frustration might have made her smile. "Then get her in the car, and let's get out of here."

A windshield two cars over shattered beneath a gunshot, and she dove into the back seat.

Chase slammed the door shut behind her and got off three shots before jumping into the driver's side. She barely had both herself and the child buckled into seat belts before the vehicle lurched forward, tires screeching as he whipped around and shot out of the parking lot.

The child hugged her knees against her chest and lowered her head.

Diana gripped the assist handle above the door with one hand, and flung the other out in front of the little girl to keep her pressed against the seat, ignoring the way her shoulder begged for relief. She tightened her grip and looked out the back window. "They're coming. A dark gray sedan just whipped out of the lot."

"Even if their car just happened to be parked right there by the edge of the lot, that's too fast for them to have gotten off the roof, to the vehicle and pulled out. There must be more than just the two shooters." He drove with one eye on the rearview mirror and one scanning for an escape route. "What the h—"

"Hey!" She shot him a dirty look in the rearview mirror.

He stared back at her, those ice-blue eyes unnerving, as he whipped around the corner to the right and started up the mountain. "What *in the world* did you witness out at that fire?"

She ran back through the memories while he tried to put some distance between them and the car pursuing them. No easy task on a road that wove up the mountain for miles with no turnoffs. "Nothing that should warrant this."

He glanced over his shoulder at the child, opened his mouth as if about to question her, then decided against it and returned his gaze to the winding mountain road.

It seemed his concern for the little girl's well-being even came before getting answers. She couldn't help but wonder if he was as jaded toward children as he appeared to be.

The car seemed inclined to follow at a cautious distance, as the attackers were probably waiting until the road widened and the driver could renew his assault without risking losing control.

Diana tried again to picture the scene at the cabin—the man had been shot, as had the woman. The child behind the chair was unconscious, or pretending to be. Had the shooter even known she was there? It had been the middle of the night, so why hadn't she been in bed instead of fully dressed, including sneakers?

Chase frowned in the rearview mirror, pulling her focus back to the present.

"What's wrong?" She turned and looked behind her, but the car was gone. "Where'd they go?"

"They just made a three-point turn and took off in the opposite direction."

She turned back to face him in the mirror. "Why doesn't that comfort me?"

"I don't know." He shook his head. "But I feel the same way."

Wow. Finally, something the two of them could agree on. Movement a little way up the mountain ahead of them on their left grabbed her attention. An animal? A person? She wasn't sure. A low rumble vibrated through the car as a section of stone gave way and sent a wave of rocks and debris crashing down the side of the mountain.

"Hold on to her!"

Diana barely had a chance to register the rockslide before a giant boulder slammed into the driver's side. She pulled her arm from the shoulder harness, leaving the lap belt in place, and flung her body across the child, gripping the back seat on either side of the little girl to brace her.

Another loud crash, followed by squealing tires as Chase struggled and failed to regain control. Her seat belt held as the car tipped precariously over the edge, teetering above the ravine that plunged down the mountainside. Even as Diana closed her eyes and prayed, the next barrage sent them over the edge.

Chase didn't have time to assess himself for injuries, so he ignored whatever pain tried to intrude. They'd come to rest partway down the hillside, wedged between two trees, one of them a sturdy pine, the other a sapling bent almost to the point of snapping. If that happened, it would send them tumbling the rest of the way down. Rocks, pebbles and dirt pelted the car. "Are you okay?"

"Yes."

Not wanting to move and endanger them further—as if they could be in any more danger than hanging off the side of a ledge while an untold number of gunmen plotted to finish the job they'd started—he shifted his gaze to the rearview mirror.

Diana seemed to be telling the truth. Though he could see the pain in her expression clearly enough, she was already gingerly examining the little girl even as her gaze darted around to assess the situation. While her determined demeanor had so far grated on his nerves when she questioned his every move, having a strong partner he wouldn't have to coddle or shield might actually come in handy under the current circumstances.

He shifted his attention to the child. The fact that she hadn't so much as cried out once during the time she'd been with them had him concerned, but that was a problem for a later time. Right now...

"We have to get out of here before any more of that mountain gives way." The slide seemed to have paused for the moment, but their vehicle would only cling to the mountainside with debris weighing them down for so long, even with the trees offering support. "Can you unbuckle the belts?"

"Yes." She unbuckled herself, then spoke in the little girl's ear, the words too soft for him to hear. Whatever she'd said worked, because the child wrapped her arms around Diana's neck and clung tightly while Diana freed her from the lap belt. "Which way?"

He hit the buttons to roll down his window and the back

window directly behind his. "Driver's side. Onto the debris pile and off toward the front of the vehicle."

She looked down the mountain out the kid's window, seemed to contemplate their options, then slid across the seat and glanced out the window he'd opened.

"Is that okay with you?"

She either missed his sarcasm or chose to ignore it. "Without equipment, it's probably the best option. Though, we'll have to move fast to get out of the path before any more debris comes tumbling down."

"Works for me." He was just glad she was being agreeable for once. He unhooked his belt and set it gingerly aside, then paused. The child was a little slip of a thing, and Diana probably didn't top 110 pounds soaking wet, while he weighed in at a solid 220. There'd be more of a chance the vehicle would shift with the movement of his weight than theirs. "Can you get the girl out on your own?"

She lifted an eyebrow at him, then frowned, concern etched deeply in her features. "You okay?"

He met her gaze in the mirror, willing her to understand his concerns, or at least accept his decision, without him having to spell it out and risk frightening the child further. "I'm fine. I just think it would be best if you two *moved* first."

Her eyes widened with understanding, and the fear reflected there mirrored his own.

"Go. Now."

She nodded. "Okay. Honey, I'm going to help you climb out the window. Okay?"

As far as Chase could hear, the girl didn't respond, but he could no longer see them since Diana had shifted behind his seat when she'd moved closer to the window.

"Once I put you out, you stay right there and wait for me. Don't move. Okay?"

He waited, but still heard no response. Chase had grown up going to church every Sunday and religious instruction on Saturdays, had even clung to his faith as an adult, but he'd given up on praying after Victoria and the child they'd been trying to protect had been murdered...despite all of Chase's prayers for their safety. But now, for the first time in close to eight years, he closed his eyes and uttered a prayer—not for himself, which would be hypocritical, but for the little girl who'd already suffered so much trauma and the woman who seemed willing to risk everything to protect her.

"Okay, she's out." Diana's voice yanked him back to the reality of their situation.

Chase opened his eyes and watched the child curl into a ball beside the car in his sideview mirror. "Your turn."

She inhaled deeply. "I'll try not to shift anything."

He laughed to himself. "Good idea."

Deep, husky laughter filled the car. "Didn't anyone ever tell you no one likes a smart aleck?"

He couldn't help but grin. His boss, Zac Jameson, often called him the same thing. "Maybe once or twice."

"Okay, here goes." She moved slowly, gingerly, taking her time to shift her weight, waiting between moves to be sure they weren't going to tumble down the side of the mountain. As she edged out the window, the mountain groaned, but didn't start to slide...yet. "I'm out," she announced.

"Get the girl out of the way!" He waited until she scooped up the child and carried her off the rock pile, then started to move. He could see his cell phone lying in the passen-

ger side footwell, ached to reach over and grab it. He didn't
know if Diana had hers, and without it they'd be stranded
on the side of the mountain with no way to summon help.

The decision was made for him when the sapling gave
out beneath the car's weight. He yanked his feet onto the
seat, braced himself and dove out the window even as the
car began its descent down the mountainside, taking the
debris pile jammed behind it along with it. He scrambled
for purchase, searching for some kind of solid ground to
grab on to as he rolled to the side.

"Grab my hand!"

As the debris shifted and slid beneath him, he reached
out blindly for the sound, and found a delicate hand.

He grabbed hold of the tether, which was much stronger
than he'd first thought, and threw himself toward her. The
anchor slowed him enough to catch a massive pine just past
the one Diana had braced herself against. He pulled himself
up to her, and wedged Diana and the child between him
and the tree. Turning his back on the slide, he wrapped his
arms around Diana, the child and the tree trunk, ducked
his head to keep from getting pummeled by stray debris
and held on for dear life.

He choked on the dirt that kicked up as he waited for
everything to once again settle. When it finally did, he
lifted his head and examined the little girl, head tucked
beneath Diana's chin, hands clamped rigidly over her ears
to drown out the roar.

Diana lifted her head, cradling the child in a firm grip
as she met Chase's eyes. "You okay?"

"Yeah." He nodded and moved back a step. "You?"

"I think so. Still shaking, though."

"Me, too." He looked into her eyes. From this close, he

noticed the bursts of gold around the pupils in her brown eyes. He'd never seen anything like it before, like intense gold stars amid the brown. Even with her face covered in dust and bits of powdered rock, she was incredibly beautiful.

Then she narrowed those eyes at him and lifted her chin. "You're bleeding."

He reached up in the direction she'd indicated and swiped his temple. His hand came away bloody. Huh. A head injury. Well, that explained a lot. "I'm okay. We should move, though."

She was already shaking her head. "We can't. We have to stay near where the vehicle went over until help arrives. The mountain road is heavily traveled enough that the slide should be reported soon. Then they'll bring a chopper in to check for vehicles."

She was quite possibly the most stubborn, thickheaded, beautiful, exasperating woman he'd ever met. "Right before the slide, I saw something on the side of the mountain," he told her.

"I saw that, too. Like a shadow or something moving?"

"No, a flash of light. Maybe a flashlight." In broad daylight? "Or…something else."

She froze, her expression caught somewhere between shock and disbelief. "You think they were just watching us? Or…"

"Yeah," he acknowledged. *"Or."* It seemed outlandish that someone would have started a rockslide, timed to exactly when they were on that stretch of road…but it would explain why the other car had mysteriously stopped following them. And since the road didn't have any turnoffs, it wouldn't have been too hard to guess that this was the route they'd take. The setup would have taken manpower and equipment, and it wouldn't have been easy...but it was possible.

"Someone, it would appear, has extensive resources. And is able to mobilize them very quickly." He looked up over his shoulder, watching the dust settle, half expecting snipers to line the ridge at any moment. "Normally, I'd agree with you that we should wait until help comes. Unfortunately, these are far from normal circumstances."

She scanned the spot where he'd just been looking. "Alright. Let's move."

He had to admire the fact that once she made a decision, she didn't hesitate. Maybe that was why she was so careful to make the right decisions.

She stood, shifting the child's weight to her good arm, and clutched the other arm against her body with a hiss.

How in the world had she managed to brace the little girl's weight and hold on to the tree with her bad arm while reaching out to save him? She had to have been in an incredible amount of pain—had to still be hurting something awful. He should offer to carry the little girl, but something in him balked at the idea. He argued with himself that she was probably more comfortable with Diana, giving himself permission to take the coward's way out. He gently placed a hand on Diana's shoulder. "Thank you. If you hadn't reached out a hand, I don't know that I could have stopped myself from sliding all the way down."

She smiled. "Sure you would have. It just might have taken a little longer."

He blew out a frustrated breath. The woman even argued against gratitude. What was he supposed to do with that? Instead of standing there trying to figure it out, he started forward. They were sitting ducks where they were. They needed to get moving.

"Watch out for rattlers."

He froze. "Rattlers?"

She plowed into him. "What's wrong? Why'd you stop?"

He scanned the ground for movement, then stepped carefully into the knee-high grass. "By rattlers, you mean snakes?"

"Of course, I mean snakes. What else would a rattler be?" She frowned and shook her head as if he'd lost his mind.

Better for her to think he didn't understand the reference than to let her know the truth—that he was terrified of snakes, had been ever since he'd been bitten when he was a child. Wouldn't want her to think the big, bad bodyguard who'd been sent to protect the child was a coward. Only when it came to snakes, but still. "Sorry. I grew up on Long Island. Not many rattlesnakes there."

"Not many bears, either, I suppose?"

"Nope. I guess they don't like crossing the bridges."

She dug her fingers into his arm hard enough to bruise. "Hey—"

He froze in his tracks as a massive black bear crashed through the brush straight into their path.

THREE

Diana froze, her gaze caught on the massive animal blocking their path.

The little girl gripped her neck so tight she almost strangled her.

Chase stood perfectly still and barely breathed. "If we don't move, will it keep going?"

"Hard to tell," she whispered just as quietly. "The rockslide probably spooked him."

The bear stood watching them.

Chase's breathing grew harsher. "We can't just stand here in the open."

"With targets on our backs?" Courtesy of however many gunmen might be lining up on the ridge right now.

"Exactly."

He was right. She had to force herself not to turn and look over her shoulder. They were too exposed in the clearing. And whoever had caused that rockslide could be anywhere. Too bad the agitated black bear was standing between them and the relative concealment of the forest.

Chase slid his weapon from its holster and lifted it toward the animal.

Diana reached out and put a hand over his. "No. It's not necessary yet and might draw unwanted attention."

"So what do you suggest?" Even though he lowered the pistol, he didn't reholster it.

"Can you take her from me? Slowly?"

When he didn't immediately answer, she risked glancing in his direction. If possible, he looked more horrified by the prospect of taking the child than he did of taking on the bear. Under other circumstances, she might have been amused.

"If my hands are full, I won't be able to shoot." He lifted his chin toward the ridge above them.

As if she needed the reminder there were assassins after them. The bear, while a more immediate threat, was actually the least of their problems. If they could just get around him, he'd probably move on rather than stalk them through the forest. "You can get her to the safety of the woods while I distract the bear."

"Dis…" His breath rushed out in a whoosh. "No. Absolutely not. Think of a plan B."

"I have no plan B."

The bear roared and shook his head.

The little girl slapped her hands over her ears, finally releasing her death grip on Diana's neck.

Diana sucked in a deep, greedy breath of the cool autumn air. Everything she knew about bears ran through her head. And she dismissed every idea just as quickly, since they all involved making noise, which might help with one threat but might just as easily bring a more deadly one. At least one or two of them had a chance of escaping the bear. If the gunmen reappeared on the ridge while they still stood in the clearing, they could pick them all off at their leisure.

"What if we play dead?" Chase asked.

"No. Not with a black bear." She looked around the clearing for anything that could be used as a weapon and wouldn't make noise. There were plenty of rocks but not much else. "See if you can slowly crouch down and pick up some rocks."

"Rocks? You want me to fight a bear with rocks?"

"You're not going to fight him, just try to scare him off." She spared him her best scathing glare. "Unless you have a better idea?"

"We'll try your way first." He finally reholstered the weapon. "Be ready to run. And make sure you run behind me, not between me and him."

"Okay."

Chase bent his knees and moved painstakingly slowly, gaze riveted on the bear.

Without warning, the animal charged.

"Go! Run!" Before he even finished the words, he had the weapon back in his hand. He fired off three shots as Diana backpedaled, with him behind her covering their backs.

All three shots went wide, two tearing through the forest on either side of the charging animal, the third ricocheting off a tree. Either he was a lousy shot, or he'd deliberately missed the three-hundred-pound target not fifty feet in front of him. She doubted Chase Mitchell missed anything he aimed at.

Diana turned and ran, pain throbbing through her shoulder and all the way down her wrist. Holding on to the child who kept her hands clamped over her ears was difficult, throwing off her balance.

"Hey. Stop," Chase huffed. "It's okay."

She paused and glanced back over her shoulder.

Chase waited for her to stop, then bent at the waist, hands on his knees as he still clutched the gun, and sucked in deep lungfuls of the crisp air. "It's safe. The ricochet grazed him, and he took off the other way."

Diana squeezed her eyes closed for just a moment and uttered a silent thank-you, too winded to get the words out.

"But we can't stay here long."

She nodded, inhaling slowly through her nose, and blowing out through her mouth in an effort to regulate her breathing.

"Let me know as soon as you can move." He looked her in the eye. "They'll know that we survived the crash now, if they didn't before."

She nodded, not ready to move but knowing they had no choice. Without a word, she started forward, concentrating on slowing her breathing and staying on her feet.

They hiked along the slope parallel to the road in silence, using the thick forest as cover. Diana's shoulder begged her to rest as pain pounded through her head. Carrying the little girl's weight on one hip while she struggled to walk on the uneven ground had her nearly whimpering, and still she trudged on, one step after another. But the fact that the little girl hung limply in her arms, no longer responding to Diana—not even when she directed the girl to hold on while she navigated a particularly difficult section of roots and brush—was what finally drove her to stop. "Chase."

"Yeah?" He paused, turned to her from a few feet ahead, did an automatic scan of the area.

"We're going to have to stop for a few minutes."

He walked back to her. "Are you okay?"

"Yes. It's not me. I need to assess her condition." Diana lowered the little girl into a pile of leaves.

Chase stood over her, hands on his hips, attention split between the child and their surroundings. "Is something wrong?"

She glanced up at him and lifted an eyebrow. Had he seriously just asked her that?

"Alright. Fair enough." He shot her an adorably sheepish grin then sobered almost immediately. "Seriously, though, is she okay?"

"I don't know—that's why I need to check." She winced a little at just how harsh her voice sounded. Then she sighed and tucked strands of her hair, which were limp and covered in dust and pebbles, behind her ears before she started to examine the girl. "I'm sorry. I'm exhausted, in pain and not at my best."

"Actually, you've been fantastic." His eyes widened, and Diana wasn't sure who was more surprised by the compliment, him or her.

"Thank you." Not sure what else to say, she changed the subject. "Do you think it's safe to start angling up toward the road now, see if we can get cell-phone service?"

He studied her a moment longer, then looked around. "Probably as safe as it's going to get."

Diana understood the implied warning. "I wouldn't ask, but we need to get her somewhere safe and warm and have a doctor examine her."

The little girl's eyes shot open.

As Diana had suspected, she'd been playing possum, listening and absorbing every word.

Diana kneeled down so that she was face-to-face with her, trusting Chase—as difficult as it was—to keep an eye out. She smoothed the little girl's hair out of her face and brushed some of the dust and dirt from her cheeks. "Honey,

I already told you my name, and you know this is Chase, but we don't know what to call you. I promise I'm not going to push you to talk about anything you're not ready to talk about, but could you just tell me your name so we know what to call you?"

She hesitated, her jade-colored eyes wide with fear.

"Please, honey. Chase and I are trying to keep you safe. We're not going to hurt you, and we're not going to let anyone else hurt you." She tried to put a firm note into her tone. She didn't want to scare the little girl, but pleading had so far gotten her nowhere. "I just want to know your name. And maybe how old you are. Can you tell me that?"

The child glanced at Chase, then back at Diana, the deer-in-the-headlights look still firmly in place. Finally, she whispered so softly Diana had to strain to hear her. "Emmie. I not supposta talk to strangers."

Giving herself a moment to swallow the lump clogging her throat, Diana moved to sit beside Emmie. She wrapped an arm around her shoulders and pulled her against her side, as if holding her close could shelter her from any danger that might come. "It's very nice to meet you, Emmie. And you're right. You shouldn't talk to strangers. Did your mommy teach you that?"

Emmie nodded, sniffling.

Diana couldn't help but think of the woman she'd found in the fire. She'd pray it wasn't Emmie's mother, even though deep down she'd already accepted the fact that she most likely was. What else would Emmie have been doing with her and the man in a cabin in the woods in the middle of the night? Unfortunately, there were difficult questions that were going to need to be asked soon enough. For now, she just wanted to ascertain Emmie's condition and get her somewhere safe. "Did Mommy also teach you that it was okay to talk to firefighters and police officers?"

Emmie turned to look at her, then tilted her head and sniffed. "Y-y-yes."

"Well, then it's okay to talk to us. I'm a firefighter, and Chase is, uh…a policeman." As far as a two- or three-year-old would understand his role, anyway. She didn't want to lie to her, but at the same time, she needed her to feel safe. "And we are going to take care of you until we can get you back to your family."

"I want Mommy," she sobbed and threw herself into Diana's arms.

Ignoring the agony tearing through her, Diana pulled her close and hugged her, resting her cheek on Emmie's head. "I know you do, honey. It's okay. We're going to figure everything out. I promise. But first we have to get somewhere warmer, okay?"

Emmie nodded, rocking back and forth.

"I'm just going to ask you a few questions so I can help you. Would that be all right?"

She hesitated, sniffed. "Uh-huh."

"You don't have to answer anything you're uncomfortable with."

Chase shifted from foot to foot, his patience clearly waning. Well, too bad. He'd just have to deal. They'd be on the move again soon enough. She sighed. Not that she could really blame him for being impatient, considering there were apparently trained assassins on their heels…

Which they were going to have to discuss at some point, but not while Emmie could hear. But, as she bit back the urge to ask his thoughts on the situation, her own edginess began to grow. The urgency to move beat at her. And

Diana had learned long ago to trust her instincts. "Do you hurt anywhere, Emmie?"

Emmie nodded.

Chase leaned closer over Diana's shoulder as she set Emmie back in the leaf pile and kneeled to examine her. "What hurts?"

"My head." She touched a lump on her forehead that had already begun to bruise. "And here and here." First, she gripped her arm, then her leg.

Diana took the time to examine her. Something had scraped her shin up to her knee, but it was a shallow scrape that had already stopped bleeding. It would probably be okay as long as they could get it cleaned out soon. Her arm, on the other hand, needed an X-ray. Diana didn't think it was broken, but she couldn't be sure. She pushed Emmie's sleeve up higher and noticed a pattern of bruising. If she wasn't mistaken, which she very clearly wasn't, someone had grabbed her by the arm with enough force to leave finger-mark bruises. Rage surged through her as she leaned to the side and glanced up at Chase.

Chase shrugged off his flannel shirt, leaving him in only a short-sleeved, gray T-shirt. His jaw firmed as he clenched his teeth and squatted beside them, then tucked the flannel around Emmie's shoulders. "Did—"

"Emmie..." She gave him a discreet headshake. She could tell what he wanted to ask, but this wasn't the time or place for this discussion. They had to get to safety first. Besides, if they pushed her for answers too soon, she might shut down altogether. Better to wait until they could have a therapist present before questioning her about what had happened.

He nodded his understanding.

"Okay, then. Let's go." Grateful that Emmie seemed to be coming around, and wasn't as detached as she'd been, Diana stood and picked her up.

When they started forward again, Chase taking up the lead, he began to angle upward, using trees, branches and saplings to brace himself, reaching back to help Emmie and Diana through the steeper inclines. Diana had given him her cell phone, and he checked it every now and then in hopes of getting service. When he finally did, he breathed a sigh of relief and stood perfectly still. "We have service. What do you want to do?"

She resisted the urge to look over her shoulder to see if he was talking to someone else. Who knew? Perhaps she'd earned an iota of trust over the past few hours. "With that rockslide wiping out a good part of the road, it'll be a while before any rescue vehicles can make it up here, and there's nowhere to land a chopper that we could walk to before dark, not in our current conditions."

He nodded and looked around, clearly having already come to the same conclusion.

Grateful for the momentary respite, Diana set down Emmie and stretched her back, then took a minute to get her bearings. She knew the terrain well, had hiked it hundreds of times over the past four years in an effort to outrun the memories that tormented her, the images that followed her into sleep each night and the screams that ripped her from those nightmares. It hadn't worked, but at least she now knew the area. "There's a hunting cabin a couple of miles from here. It belongs to a friend of mine."

He glanced at Emmie and lifted his brow. "Uphill?"

"Only a little. It's right off the road, so only up the kind of long driveway." A hike she dreaded already, but since they had so few options, she forced the thought from her mind, for now. "He's a fellow firefighter, and I know he leaves a key because he rents the cabin out. All I have to do is call, and he'll tell me where to find it."

Chase pursed his lips, then narrowed his gaze as he studied the terrain. "You trust him?"

She started to say "of course," then checked the urge. Did she? Honestly, she didn't fully trust anyone. "I don't see how he'd be involved in any of this. But either way, there's an SUV in the garage as well. At worst, we'll be able to use it to leave."

"Fair enough." He held the phone out to her. "But I'm still going to have to call my boss and see if he'll arrange for a doctor for Emmie."

While she'd have felt safer holed up in the mountain retreat with no one else around, she couldn't argue the fact that Emmie needed more care than she and her brooding companion could provide. Yet, when she tried to agree, the words refused to come out, so she simply nodded, took the phone from him and called Harrison Rhodes.

"Make sure he doesn't tell anyone we'll be staying there."

She nodded and scanned her surroundings just as the phone started to ring. They'd stay still long enough to make the calls to Harrison, Naomi—to let her know what was going on—and Chase's boss, to make arrangements, but then they'd have to move.

Her shoulder and back screamed in protest at the thought. She ignored them both. Her discomfort was the least of their problems. She could only hope the bear was long gone and that no one with semiautomatic weapons was hanging around.

* * *

Diana carried Emmie without complaint. She waited until Emmie went limp, her soft rhythmic breaths assuring she'd fallen asleep, then kept her voice low. "What do you make of all of this?"

"You're sure she's asleep, right?" Chase asked—what did he know about kids? This one seemed to play possum on a regular basis—a coping mechanism, he assumed.

Diana looked down at Emmie and nodded. "Yeah, she's beat. Out like a light."

He stopped for a minute beside a large boulder, gesturing for Diana to lean against it. At the moment, the forest was thick enough to offer protection from snipers, so they could take a break. He stretched. His muscles ached, especially his back, where he'd been shot trying to save the last child he'd been charged with protecting. The pain he felt on overexertion served as a constant reminder that he'd failed. "I'm not sure what to think. It definitely seemed like the gunmen at the hospital were intent on killing the two of you."

"But why?" She shook her head.

She looked so lost, so fragile, in that moment, he wanted to reach out and—and what? Reassure her? Lie to her? Tell her everything would be okay when there was a better than good chance it wouldn't be? Besides, as vulnerable as she might seem leaning against that boulder with the child tucked against her, Diana Cameron struck him as anything but breakable.

"I don't know. But we need to figure it out." The most likely explanation was that the child had witnessed something, but... "If they wanted Emmie dead, why not shoot her at the scene like they did with her parents? Even with the fire, why let her live when there was a chance she could get out?"

"Honestly, I can't make sense of it, and I've tried. Both adults in the room had been shot before I arrived. The first explosion happened while I was still in my Jeep. Yet, Emmie was not only alive by the time I got into the cabin, but unharmed, as far as I can tell, and the doctors confirmed that much at the hospital before we were forced to flee." Diana shrugged as best she could with a limp Emmie in her arms. "Why leave her in the fire to die? Why not either kill her or take her with them?"

And then it dawned on him. "You said you found her behind an armchair in the corner of the living room?"

She frowned. "Yes."

"And the man and the woman, presumably her parents, were in the same room?"

"Uh-huh."

He studied the child. Even in sleep, she didn't appear to be at peace. He lowered his voice to a whisper. "She hid from the killer."

Diana's expression remained neutral. Apparently, she'd already considered the same theory. "Her mother was scared. She might have told her to hide if anyone came to the house. I think maybe whoever killed her mother and father and then set the fire didn't know she was there—not until he saw me go into the house and come out with her."

That made the most sense to him as well. But…something nagged at him. It took a minute before he could place it, but finally the image became clear in his mind. The gunmen at the hospital. When they burst into the room, they hadn't just been carrying guns.

"The men who came into the hospital room…" he said

to Diana. "I only caught a glimpse, but I'm pretty sure one of them was carrying zip ties and a cloth, maybe to use as a gag?"

Diana's eyes went wide with horror. "You don't mean…"

He nodded sharply. "I think they were trying to abduct her."

"So they're not trying to kill her, only whoever's protecting her."

"Yeah. At least, that's what I figure. For whatever reason, whoever is trying to kill us is trying to abduct Emmie. They might have shot the man and the woman to get to her."

The thought had his blood running ice-cold. No way would anyone get their hands on this child while he still had breath in his body. "Maybe the man you found in the cabin wasn't her father. Maybe he was with her mother for whatever reason, maybe an affair, and her father killed them both and tried to grab Emmie."

"But why set the fire? It could have easily killed Emmie."

"The mother might have lied, said Emmie wasn't there in an attempt to protect her. Or maybe there's something more going on here. I just don't know."

Diana winced as she shifted Emmie to her bad shoulder in order to stretch her back.

It wasn't fair that he hadn't offered to take Emmie from her yet, had allowed Diana to trudge across a mountain carrying twenty or more pounds with an injured shoulder because… Because what? Keeping his hands free to shoot if needed was only an excuse. So why was he so afraid to take the burden from her for even a few minutes? Maybe the risk of becoming attached was too great, because if he did, and then lost her like he'd lost the other child, he doubted he could make it through without breaking. He'd barely made it through the first time. "Can you fire a weapon?"

"Sure. Why?" She stiffened. "You're not leaving us here, are you?"

"What? No. No, I uh…" He gestured toward Emmie. "I can carry her for a little while, give your arm a rest."

"It's okay." She snuggled her closer. "I've got her. Besides, I'm not that good a shot."

He nodded, embarrassed to admit, even to himself, the relief that coursed through him. He gestured for her to go ahead, then started walking again, picking up the conversation as if they'd never paused. "The bruises on her arm, a handprint?"

"Yeah."

"How sure are you?"

"Positive."

"Okay." He nodded, struggling to envision the scenario. "You said the man and the woman were shot, and Emmie was behind the chair. So you have to figure, either one of the two victims put the bruises there, or someone else did, possibly the killer."

"The bruises seem pretty fresh. If the killer knew she was there in the house, why didn't he either take her with him or…" She swallowed hard. "You know. What does he want with her?"

"I don't know. But I agree with you about one thing."

"Only one?" She smirked.

A smile tugged at him, but he ignored the question. "The only thing that makes sense is that you interrupted whatever he had planned."

"So there are three questions we need answers to. One, who killed the couple? Two, who hurt Emmie? And three, what does the killer—and all the other people who seem to be working with him—want with her?"

Who was the first person he'd heard the child call for? Her mother. "Maybe the killer grabbed her by the arm, pulled her away from her mother and flung her aside, then couldn't find her afterward."

Diana tilted her head back and forth, looked up the mountain to the road not that far above them now, then hiked Emmie higher against her good shoulder. "I'm just not sure she could hide well enough to stay hidden from a grown man. Keep in mind, he wouldn't have started the fire until he was ready to leave the building. So this would have happened when there was no fire, no smoke. He wouldn't have had any trouble seeing."

"Maybe it wasn't a question of him being able to see her, but him being able to *get* to her. She might have been able to hide somewhere small enough that he couldn't reach in after her. If that's what happened, then he might have set the fire thinking it would force her to run outside, where he could grab her."

Diana nodded slowly. "That's definitely possible. I can see it having happened that way. But everything that's happened since then… Emmie and I could have both died when they fired those shots at us right after the fire. Or at the hospital. Or the rockslide could have killed us. If they want her alive, why take so many risks?"

"Maybe they'd prefer to capture her alive…but if that wasn't possible, then it's possible they'd rather have her dead than in police custody."

She frowned. "What do you mean?"

"Think about it. You showed up at the house and saved her—and then you keep saving her, over and over again. If they don't find a way to stop us, you're going to make sure Emmie feels safe enough to talk to my sister, and she'll tell the authorities everything she saw. If it really is Emmie's father behind all this, she'd be able to identify him, don't you think?" Chase had come across plenty of criminals in his time with the FBI, and he knew how they operated. Whatever this scumbag might want with Emmie, he was sure to care more about keeping himself out of jail. If that meant Emmie died, so be it.

Frankly, the fact that the little girl was still alive after all she'd been through was nearly enough to make Chase wonder if divine intervention may have played a role. He'd read the report about the initial fire, knew Diana had been on her way home, and still... "What were you doing there, anyway?"

"I'd just gotten off my shift at the firehouse, and I was exhausted. Honestly, I would usually have just bunked there instead of driving while I was that tired, but the storm was coming, and there's always a chance the lightning will start a fire, so I just really wanted to go home and sleep in my own bed for a little while before the likelihood I'd get called out again."

"Oh, yeah?" He grinned. "How'd that work out for you?"

She laughed and shook her head, then hugged Emmie closer. "It actually worked out perfectly. I might not have gotten to sleep, in my bed or anywhere else, but this child is alive because I followed the path down which God led me."

Unsure what to say to that, wishing he could find the same determined faith she seemed so at ease with, he turned the conversation back to a topic he felt safer discussing. Murder. "The only thing that makes sense, other than that he wants her for some very important nefarious purpose, is that the killer is worried that now that she's in our custody, she might talk. Otherwise, why keep coming after her? Why not cut his losses and disappear?"

Diana stopped walking and turned to face him, her expression hard. For the first time, he noticed the exhaustion she'd alluded to. Dark circles ringed her eyes. Her posture, rigid when they'd first met, sagged beneath the child's weight and the pain she must be enduring. "You think she knows the killer well enough to identify him, even if it wasn't her father."

"Yeah," he answered, though she hadn't phrased it as a question. The more he thought about it, the more sense it made. "A random stranger, unless something about him made him easily identifiable, probably wouldn't be worried a child that age could give an accurate enough description to be of concern to him."

A gentle breeze rippled her hair. "Do you think it was the killer who came after us at the hospital?"

"I'm not sure." Would it be worth the risk to show himself when he clearly wielded the resources to send a bunch of lackeys to do the job? "The way I figure it, there had to have been at least five people involved so far. The two gunmen at the hospital, the two that followed us out of the lot and whoever was on that mountainside before the rockslide, any one of whom could have killed the couple in the house. Which makes sense, if Naomi's theory is right, and organized crime or a gang are involved. I guess it depends on if their killer is the guy in charge or just a hired gun."

"Whatever is going on does seem to be pretty involved. It seems…" She frowned, suspicion darkening her gaze. "Coordinated. And they moved fast. Really fast. Almost as if they anticipated what you'd do before you even did it."

"Hey." He couldn't blame her for suspecting him when the gunmen had shown up practically on his heels. It was something he was going to have to think more about. Coincidence? Maybe. Though he didn't believe in coincidence any more than she seemed to. He gripped her arm gently, looked her in the eye. "We're going to have to at least semi-trust one another if we're going to care for this child and keep her safe."

She studied him, stared so deeply into his eyes he figured she could see all the way to his soul, all his deep, dark, terrifying secrets on display for her to examine at will. He barely resisted the urge to squirm beneath her scrutiny.

He did, however, breathe a sigh of relief when she simply said, "I guess, for now," and started walking again.

He fell into step beside her, keeping his head on a swivel to check the area for snakes, bears and gunmen, in that order. Somehow, he was going to keep this woman and child safe. Even though he'd been fully prepared to hand off this case the instant Zac could find a replacement, had only taken it on because his sister had asked—there was no way he'd walk away now. Somehow, he'd find a way to save this child. *Please, God, help me do that.*

The prayer came easier this time, more naturally, as prayer had eight years ago.

A roofline appeared over the next ridge, and Diana sighed. "There it is."

"We have to cross the road." An idea he wasn't fond of, since it would leave them exposed to anyone who might be waiting on higher ground. Given how many people seemed to be involved in all of this, it wasn't too much of a stretch to think they could be watching the roads around the crash site.

"Yes, and then there's a winding driveway."

He held out a hand to stop her. "Why don't we cross the road here, then find a spot for you to lay low with Emmie for a few minutes while I scout the area around the cabin?"

She looked toward the road, then behind them, and frowned.

"Will you be okay by yourself?" he asked.

She caught her lower lip between her teeth, then nodded. "We'll be fine."

"Okay. We'll head straight up and cross the road here, then I'll track through the woods and make sure everything's clear before I come back for you." He held out her cell phone, which he'd used to contact Naomi and Zac. "There's not much charge left, so don't use it unless you have to. But if you hear gunshots, or if I don't get back within fifteen minutes, call the last number dialed and tell Zac Jameson who you are and that you need help."

She lifted an eyebrow. "Yes, sir."

"I'm serious, Diana. Please, promise me you'll do as I ask."

"I will. *If* you don't come back or if I hear shots fired. But do you seriously think your boss has the resources to get someone through a rockslide and up this mountain to us when there's not much daylight left?"

He grinned. "It's been my experience there's not much Zac Jameson can't do."

FOUR

It didn't take Chase long to check the cabin and return for them. Diana forced herself to move forward, but the last stretch was the most difficult so far. Sitting still had allowed stiffness to creep in and settle…well, pretty much everywhere. They trudged on silently, apparently having nothing left to say to each other once they'd exhausted what they suspected, which was very little, and what they knew, which was even less, about Emmie and the murders.

Diana stumbled up the three steps to the porch of the A-frame cabin, and Chase reached out a hand to steady her, his grip on her arm firm, strong and reassuring.

She regained her balance and shook it off. "Thanks."

"Sure." Using the key he must have pocketed when he'd done his reconnaissance, he unlocked the front door and pushed it open for her to enter. "I'm just going to run the perimeter once more, then I'll be back."

"Okay."

He waited for her to move inside with Emmie, then closed the door and locked it with the key.

Diana stood in the entryway and scanned the open, but efficient, floor plan. Her gaze skipped across the living room, the seating all arranged around the beautiful stone fireplace taking up one entire wall, past the kitchen, whose wood cabinets, butcher-block countertop and rustic appliances lent a cozy feel she might have enjoyed under other circumstances, and landed on the back wall, which was comprised of windows. No curtains, no blinds, just a fully unobstructed view of the mountain. The French doors led to a large back deck and boasted a gorgeous view of the fall foliage that made her cringe. As beautiful as it was, from a security standpoint, it was a nightmare.

She was surprised Chase hadn't nixed the whole idea.

Then he sauntered into view, stood smack in the middle of the yard with his hands on his hips and stared in at her. At least, it seemed as if he did. In reality, he was more likely staring at his own reflection in the glass, surveying the mountainside behind him and wondering how he'd gotten himself into this mess.

Not that she could blame him. Naomi had mentioned that he'd come to Shady Creek for a break after a difficult case. This couldn't have been what he'd had in mind. Not that she knew anything about his plans—or anything about him at all other than his moodiness, his obvious lack of trust, his incredible good looks. Yikes. Where had that thought come from? She quickly dismissed it.

While there was no denying Chase was a good-looking guy, her interest in him went no further than how he could help her protect Emmie. After Liam, she'd never allow another man into her world, even if he was related to Naomi. Maybe especially so, since messing up with him would mean losing Naomi's friendship, too. And there was no way she'd risk that.

Naomi had been one of the first people Diana had met upon arriving in town, and they'd become instant friends.

Close friends. Close enough for Diana to recognize the pain and sadness that sometimes darkened Naomi's eyes, probably the mirror image of her own. Neither of them had ever talked about their pasts, content to move forward without acknowledging whatever tragedies each of them may have suffered.

She shook off thoughts of Naomi and moved slowly across the floor, trying to keep Emmie from waking just yet, at least until Diana could get cleaned up and take stock of what they'd need.

Dreading the pang of pain she knew would surface when she bent to lay Emmie down, she surveyed the room. Where should she put her? The living room boasted a couch, love seat and armchair with an oversized ottoman. According to Harrison's description, the only bedroom was up a spiral wrought-iron staircase that would be difficult to navigate with a child in her arms. And, anyway, it was in a small loft area with no exits. That wouldn't be safe should someone find them.

She crossed the few steps to the love seat and lowered Emmie onto the leather cushion. It was probably best to keep her close, just in case she woke frightened.

Emmie whimpered and rolled into the corner, pulled her knees to her chest and slid her thumb into her mouth. It only took a moment for her breathing to level out. Hopefully, she'd sleep for a while longer.

A soft knock on the door had Diana's heart lurching into her chest, and she whirled toward the sound.

Chase entered then stopped short. "Sorry. I didn't mean to startle you."

"No, no." She swiped her tangled hair out of her eyes. "It's okay. My nerves are just a bit on edge."

"That's certainly understandable." He closed the door and locked it behind him, then simply stood there. "That back wall is not ideal."

To say the least.

"No." She returned her gaze to the wall of windows, then sighed and turned back to face him. "I'm sorry. I've heard Harrison talk about this place, but I've never been here before, so I didn't know."

He shrugged as if it didn't matter, when she knew full well it did. "We'll manage."

She stared at the cozy living room, the massive fireplace, wood already stacked beside it, and wished things were different, wished they weren't on the run, wished they weren't responsible for a traumatized little girl who'd probably witnessed way more than anyone ever should. When her gaze fell on Emmie, sleeping fitfully, she recognized a kindred spirit, much like Naomi…and maybe Chase, if she let herself see past his rough exterior. "As much as I'd love to light a fire in that fireplace tonight, I guess it's out of the question, huh?"

"Sorry." He gestured toward a door in the far corner of the room she could only assume was the bathroom. "Why don't you go ahead and get cleaned up while I see if I can put together something to eat?"

Just when she thought she had the brooding, alpha male all figured out. "You can cook?"

His boyish grin, charming if she was being honest with herself, allowed her a small peek into the man he might have been if whatever he'd suffered hadn't changed him. She didn't know much about him or his past. Naomi hadn't been any more forthcoming about his past than she had about her own, but she did say he'd suffered more than his share of pain and guilt.

A notification dinged on her phone, pulling her from thoughts that brought her too close to her own history for comfort. She pulled it out of her pocket and punched in the password. "It's a text from Naomi."

Chase moved closer, his woodsy scent, a combination of pine, dried leaves and fresh air, enveloping her as he leaned in to read over her shoulder. "The driver's license they found was a forgery."

"What does that mean?" She read the text again.

He shifted away from her and glanced at Emmie. "Unfortunately for her, it probably means she'll have to answer questions sooner rather than later."

Another text came in, and she shifted farther from Chase's hulking presence and read aloud. "It says here there's been no missing-persons reports filed for a child matching Emmie's description, but she'll keep checking."

"There probably wouldn't be if the two people killed were her parents."

"Or if the killer was her father."

"True." He studied Emmie another moment, then shook his head and stalked to the kitchen.

Diana leaned over, then smoothed Emmie's hair back off her face.

The sound of cabinets and drawers opening and closing reminded her she wasn't alone in this, no matter how daunting the situation might seem.

"The cabin is actually fairly well stocked." Chase splayed his hands and leaned forward on the rustic, butcher-block countertop of the island that separated the kitchen from the living room. "You're not a vegetarian or anything, are you?"

"Nope."

"Good, because there's ground beef dated a month ago in the freezer and a pretty full pantry. I could do either chili or pasta with meat sauce. Do you have a preference?"

Her stomach growled, and she laughed as she put a hand over it. "I don't, but I imagine a two- or three-year-old would probably prefer the pasta."

"Pasta it is then."

Instead of heading straight for the bathroom, Diana slid onto a stool on the living-room side of the island and watched him through the cutout. She told herself she was enjoying the chance to just be still for a few minutes, which was true, to a certain extent. But she was loathe to leave Emmie alone to go get cleaned up. What if she woke, scared and alone? Sure, Chase was there, but his skill with kids seemed to be nonexistent.

He seemed at home enough in the kitchen, though, collecting the ingredients he'd need as if he'd done so hundreds of times before. The fact that he seemed so comfortable, even in an unfamiliar kitchen while on the run, also showed he was adaptable, a good quality in Diana's eyes.

He dumped the ground beef into a saucepan on low to thaw, set out a variety of spices, took frozen garlic bread from the freezer and put it on the counter. He worked with an efficiency that told her he'd spent more than his fair share of time in kitchens, which surprised her, considering Naomi lived on whatever she could scrounge together. Thankfully, the small corner market made soup and sandwiches, or she and Diana might both have starved to death by now. "You like to cook?"

"Don't sound so surprised." He waggled his eyebrows, playful in a way she'd yet to see. "What? Men can't cook?"

Heat flared in her cheeks. "Actually, I know a number of male firefighters who are excellent cooks. But Naomi—"

A laugh boomed out before she could even finish the sentence. "Whatever you do, do not eat anything that woman cooks."

"She cooks?" Because that was news to Diana.

"If you want to call it that. Though, to be fair, she can usually manage a box of macaroni and cheese all right, if watery and soggy appeals to you."

That sounded about right. She eyed the meat starting to sizzle in the pan. "And you're better?"

"Honey, I am a gourmet chef compared to her. Though, in all honesty, there are a few foods I enjoy and cook well. The rest…" He shrugged. "Why bother making life complicated? I usually don't really care what I eat."

Now that, she could relate to.

He hesitated, studied her for a few minutes while he added spices. "You and Naomi seem close."

"We are, yes. She helped me through a difficult time when I first moved here, has been there for me ever since."

"Yeah." He smiled, his expression softening as he thought of his sister. "That sounds like her. But she's picky about her friendships. If she didn't genuinely like you, she would still have helped you, but she wouldn't have let you get close."

Diana shifted on the stool, uncomfortable with the direction this conversation was headed. "Listen, Chase. I don't know what went on in Naomi's past. It's clear she suffered some kind of pain, but she's never opened up about it, and I don't pry."

He nodded, suddenly intently fascinated with watching the meat cook. "Has she ever talked about me?"

Why did that seem like a loaded question?

"A little. She's said how you two were close growing up, how she still feels that way about you, but you've become distant over the years, tend to live out of hotel rooms and only show up only when you are completely exhausted and…" She hesitated, wondering how much to repeat. But, honestly, she didn't know all that much, anyway. "Need to recharge, I guess."

He spread his hands on the counter, his shoulders slumping beneath whatever burdened him. "It's not that I don't love my sister, or that we're not close. I do, and we are. It's just… I…"

He paused, searched through the few drawers until he came up with a can opener, then opened several cans of sauce he'd put on the counter.

"You know, I couldn't help but notice how concerned you are about Emmie's safety, not only keeping her safe from whoever is after her, but also your concern for her well-being. So, what is it that makes you shy away from her?" His hesitation before offering to carry Emmie hadn't escaped her attention. Nor had his decision not to question the little girl when they most definitely needed answers. Somehow, she had a feeling there was more to it than just a discomfort around children.

She swiveled back and forth on the stool, her attention bouncing between him, the yard and Emmie, giving him time to compose his thoughts, to decide how much to share with her and what to keep hidden. For a moment, she wished she could take the question back. It had slipped out in a moment of camaraderie, but she of all people should know better.

"Did Naomi tell you I was married?"

Her heart stuttered, her stomach pitched as if she was on a roller coaster and her full focus riveted on him. But why should this piece of news matter to her? It's not like she was interested in him, other than as a bodyguard, and possibly, one day, a friend. "You are?"

"Was." He finished opening the cans and set them beside the stove, then broke up more of the meat, leaned over and inhaled the spicy aroma. Finally, he turned to face her, leaned back against the counter and folded his arms over his chest. "I don't usually talk about what happened, but I feel like I owe you an explanation. Or, as much of one as I'm able to give, anyway."

"An explanation for what?"

"For why I allowed you to trudge up a mountain, injured, bearing the entire burden of carrying Emmie." His jaw clenched hard.

She bristled at him using the word *allow* but decided to cut him a break, since he seemed genuinely upset about the whole thing. "If I remember correctly, you offered to take her from me." Albeit hesitantly.

"Yeah." He smiled, but it held no humor, only pain. "Eventually. And I didn't argue when you said no."

"It's fine." She shrugged, trying to offer him an out that might not make him feel like he owed her anything. "I understand some people just aren't into kids."

"It's not that. I've actually always loved kids, and I was really good with them. Once up on a time, anyway." This time, when he shifted his gaze away from her, she couldn't help but note the tears shimmering in his eyes. "My wife and I were both FBI agents. We weren't usually partners, but on one particular case, there were extenuating circumstances, a child in need of protection."

Diana's stomach roiled, and a wave of nausea threatened. She could barely keep from begging him not to share a story that could only have ended in tragedy.

"That was our sole responsibility, keep that little boy safe." His breathing hitched. "And we failed."

Her heart ached for him, and she couldn't help but ask, needed to know no matter how badly she didn't want to. Maybe even as badly as he needed to tell it. "What happened?"

He reached behind himself, as if by instinct. "I was shot in the back—"

She gasped, pressed her fingers against her lips.

"Victoria was killed." The tears tipped over, rolled down his cheeks. "And we lost the little boy."

"Oh, no, Chase. I don't know what to say. I am so sorry." She fought tears of her own, knowing firsthand the guilt he would have experienced, the way he'd replay everything over and over in his mind, searching for a way it could have ended differently, the pain each and every time he realized there was no going back to change the outcome.

She stood, rounded the island and walked to him. When she was face-to-face with him, she lifted his chin until he met her gaze, then stood on her tiptoes, wrapped her arms around his neck and hugged him, his tears cool against her cheek as he clung to her. Then she stepped back and looked him straight in the eye. "That is not going to happen this time, Chase."

He nodded and swiped at his cheeks, then lowered his gaze to the counter.

"Hey." She leaned over and tilted her head so she could look up at him, will him to believe what she was telling him. "It won't, because we won't let it."

"I sure hope you're right." His gaze slid past her, and he forced a smile that didn't reach his eyes. "Looks like someone's up."

Diana turned to find Emmie sitting up on the couch, thumb in her mouth, quietly watching them. Looked like any more talking would have to wait until later. That was alright. She had a feeling Chase could use a break, anyway. She always needed one after talking about her past. Which was why she so seldomly did, at least, since she'd given up on counseling. She placed a hand against his. "Why don't I go get Emmie and myself cleaned up, and then I'll set the table for dinner."

He nodded. "Yeah, thanks."

"Sure thing." She left him to torture himself over things he couldn't change and the fear of whatever might be coming.

Dinner was quiet. The three of them sat in silence throughout the meal, mostly pushing their food around their plates. Afterward, Chase left to walk the perimeter again while Diana cleaned up and then settled Emmie back on the love seat. They had no toys for her to play with, no TV for her to watch and no way to coax any information out of her, so the little girl simply sat quietly and stared distantly into some past he and Diana weren't privy to, or dozed on and off. Not that he knew much about kids, but her behavior didn't seem healthy, and when he'd cornered Diana and asked her opinion after dinner, she'd studied Emmie and agreed.

He'd left Diana's phone in the house while he took his walk, in case anything happened and she needed to summon help. It was a decision he regretted at the moment.

He'd already spoken very briefly to Zac, and a doctor would reach them sometime tomorrow, but Chase had an uneasy feeling in his gut, a feeling he'd learned the hard way not to ignore.

Zac had also offered to set up a safe house, but Diana had balked. Though her argument that it was safer to stay put rather than risk moving tonight made sense, he had a feeling there was more to her unwillingness to let Zac help them. To say the woman seemed to have trust issues was an understatement.

He surveyed the yard. All seemed quiet. But still...

He'd left the outside lights off and turned all but one lamp off inside, which he would extinguish the instant Emmie fell asleep again. As much as he hated the idea of her waking in the dark, even a small amount of light could attract unwanted attention.

He lifted his gaze farther up the mountain, surveilling the silhouettes of trees densely packed together beneath the small amount of moonlight peeking through thickening cloud cover. Once again, he questioned his decision to spend the night at the cabin. He'd already checked the garage and found an SUV, just as Diana had said. The keys hung from a neatly labeled board in the kitchen beside the garage door. So why stay put? Because Diana was comfortable there? Because of the argument she'd made, that it was safer to stay put than to drive down the mountain in the dark, especially without knowing if the rockslide had been cleared? Even if she was right, which she probably was, something urged him to take Diana and Emmie, and flee. They could always go farther up the mountain instead. There had to be a way down the other side. Yet, in the dark, he couldn't justify risking it, no matter what his instincts said.

He sighed, his shoulders slumping with exhaustion as he trudged back toward the house. For tonight, they'd stay put. He glanced once more at the wall of windows, then shook his head, rounded the corner and headed toward the front of the house. Tomorrow would be a different story. He had no intention of keeping them in that fishbowl any longer than necessary. Diana would just have to get over whatever her problem was with allowing Zac to help them.

He stopped and rubbed the exhaustion from his eyes. Judging her wasn't fair. Diana had held up well through this entire ordeal. She'd even reached out and offered him comfort when it was clear she preferred to keep her walls up—not to mention being injured, tired, scared and feeling the weight of being responsible for a young girl who was in danger. And, considering his own trust issues, who was he to judge her? It wasn't that her opinion didn't matter, just that he knew Zac, trusted him in a way he trusted very few others. He could only pray Diana would come around, as he had.

Praying. That was new. It had been a long time since he'd prayed, yet it seemed to be coming back to him as if he'd never turned away. After losing that child, along with the woman he'd loved with all of his heart, he'd given up, had felt like God abandoned him. But had He? Or had it been the other way around?

With a sigh, he resumed his slow trek toward the house. Was he procrastinating? Maybe. Or maybe just lingering because of that uncomfortable nudge in his gut. Then again, perhaps he just didn't want to return and face Diana after he'd told her the truth about his past. Well, most of the truth, anyway.

What in the world had prodded him to open up to her? He hadn't talked to anyone about his history. Zac knew, of course, because it was a condition of employment that he know everything about his employees, but it wasn't something they really discussed. It was just something Zac needed to know so he'd never assign Chase a case protecting a child.

He climbed the few steps to the front porch, then turned and looked out over the railing down the mountainside. His eyes had mostly adjusted to the dark, yet he still didn't see any threat. His thoughts turned back to Diana.

It wasn't like she was a friend or anything—she was barely even an acquaintance. And he wasn't used to blubbering his problems all over anyone, friend or not. So why had he shared his pain with her? He told himself he owed her an explanation for his lack of chivalry, but was that all there was to it? He had no clue. This whole situation had him all messed up. Maybe he should just text Zac and see if he'd assign another agent. Chase could wash his hands of both Emmie and Diana. Naomi would just have to understand. And she would. She'd always understood him.

With that thought in mind, and one last look around, he used the key to let himself in, then closed the door behind him without making a sound…and froze. Something was wrong. His senses flared, taking in everything around him at once.

Diana's deep, even breathing from where she was lying asleep on the couch reached him. As did Emmie's tortured whimpers from her spot on the love seat, probably caused by whatever nightmares plagued her sleep. Other than that, the only other sound he could make out was the refrigerator's soft hum.

He inhaled deeply. The scent of strawberry shampoo enveloped him, overpowering the lingering aroma of the sauce they'd had for dinner.

Shadows skittered across the room as the breeze ruffled trees beneath the sliver of moonlight. One shadow stood out, deeper than the rest, darker, completely still, secreted in the far corner of the room.

Chase's heart rate ratcheted up, but he controlled his breathing, giving no outward sign of distress as he strolled across the room toward the fireplace, trying to set himself up within striking distance of whoever stood concealed in the shadows.

Diana's breathing hitched, signaling that she'd woken up, and he silently willed her not to sit up and give herself away. Once he reached his target, hopefully she'd know to grab the keys and flee with Emmie. She'd have to go up the mountain, couldn't risk heading back toward the rockslide, but she probably knew that already.

The phone was lying on the coffee table next to her. Grab it and try to casually shoot off a text to Zac? Or deal with the intruder first?

The attack came from behind with no warning, taking the decision out of his hands. A solid blow to the back of his head made him stumble and stagger forward, even as he whirled toward the second intruder he hadn't noticed.

Diana rolled from the couch onto the floor then scrambled out of sight.

Chase balled his fist and swung as he turned, connecting with a wall of rock-hard muscle.

His attacker doubled over, and Chase shoved his head

down as he rammed his knee up into the guy's face. He dropped with a grunt.

Still, Chase didn't reach for his weapon. It was too dark—it would be stupid to take a chance of firing off a shot in the small room, especially when he didn't know precisely where Diana or Emmie were.

The second guy was on him before he could even think. He hit Chase from the side, a strong right hook. These guys were no slouches—big, silent, no wasted movements. They definitely knew what they were doing. Hired muscle, if he had to guess.

Chase countered with a flurry of punches, several of which landed, backing the guy up, but only for a moment before he nailed Chase in the gut.

Chase backed off, luring the guy in closer, then kicked the side of his knee, buckling the man's leg beneath him, and followed through with a punch to the throat and another to the chin.

The guy went down hard, shattering the glass coffee table beneath him.

When a massive hand landed on his shoulder, Chase angled his elbow up and swung behind him, connecting solidly with his first attacker's jaw.

He staggered back but didn't fall.

"Down!" Diana yelled.

His attacker froze at the command, but Chase didn't hesitate, simply dropped to a crouch.

Diana hit the guy with a fireplace shovel, the clang echoing through the room as he fell, and she tossed aside the makeshift weapon.

Chase lurched to his feet and grabbed Diana's cell phone from amid the wreckage of the table. "Where's Emmie?"

Diana yanked her up from behind the couch into her arms in one fluid motion.

"Go." He shoved her toward the kitchen and pulled the gun from his holster. Now that he knew where Diana and Emmie were, he'd have no compunction about using it. "Get the keys."

She hooked them on her way into the garage, then hesitated only an instant before handing them to him and climbing into the back seat with Emmie. She had them both buckled and secured before he made it to the driver's seat.

He reholstered his weapon reluctantly, then started the SUV, an old green Wagoneer with woodgrain vinyl siding. He prayed that the vehicle would run well enough to get them out of there. He felt along the visor for an automatic garage-door opener. Thankfully, he found one and hit the button, or he'd have backed right through. As it was, he shot the Jeep backward the instant he could clear the door. He swung around, slammed the shifter into gear and smashed his foot onto the gas pedal, the abrupt change in direction bringing a wave of nausea. He fishtailed, the steering wheel spinning as he navigated the twisting driveway. "Are you two okay?" he called into the back seat, not daring to look away from the road to check on them.

"We're fine." Tremors shook Diana's voice.

There was nothing he could do for them but get them to safety. He tossed the phone back to her. "I already programmed Zac's number into the phone earlier. Text him 'urgent, need a chopper, uphill, now.' Please."

Silenced hummed through the Jeep while he waited to see if she'd do as he'd asked, and he breathed a sigh of relief when she did.

"I got the text to him, but it's just about dead."

"Turn it off." There was only one road leading up the mountain from where they were. He trusted Zac would find them. But they had to save the last bit of charge on the phone in case he needed to send directions.

She met his gaze in the rearview mirror, all of his own questions reflected in her expression. How had those men known where to find them? How had they gotten in? How had they gotten past him, for that matter? These were no amateurs they were dealing with.

And why fight instead of shooting? Were they trying to kill them, or simply trying to abduct Emmie? But this wasn't the time to discuss it. Apparently, Diana agreed, since she shifted her gaze away, then cooed softly to Emmie, desperately trying to reassure her they would keep her safe despite the dire circumstances.

Chase kept his focus straight ahead as he hardly slowed, bouncing hard over the driveway's edge onto the winding mountain road, barely nipping in front of an oncoming vehicle.

Instead of braking, the car behind them sped up and tapped their back bumper.

The Jeep's tires skidded, then regained their tentative grip on the road.

Gunfire erupted from behind them.

"Get down!" The instant the automatic-weapon fire ceased, Chase pulled his gun and held it back to Diana. "Keep your head low, cover Emmie and just aim straight out the back window at them and pull the trigger."

She grabbed the weapon, checking first that it was loaded. Good, at least she had some level of training with a pistol. "Will it rebound?"

"No, but some of the glass might spray." He held his

breath as the vehicle in pursuit increased its speed, coming for them again.

The first shot she fired echoed through the Jeep, ringing in his ears.

Emmie screamed, over and over, hands clamped over her ears as Diana tried to cover her, stay upright while Chase navigated the winding road and aim the weapon all at once.

She fired again. When the car backed off to avoid being hit, Diana tucked the weapon into her waistband and didn't bother wasting shots. "It's okay, Emmie. Everything is going to be okay. Shh, baby. I have you. You're safe now."

But there was no time for relief as the Wagoneer sputtered and wheezed, then started to slow. "One of the bullets must have hit something. We're going to have to make a run for it up the mountainside."

"Okay," Diana answered with no hesitation at all.

"Hand me the gun. I'm going to pull across the opposite side of the road as soon as I can safely do so, then dump the Jeep into the shallow ditch. You guys go out the driver's side and straight up the mountain."

"Got it." She nodded, gathered Emmie close, then met his gaze in the mirror once again. "What about you?"

"I'm going to cover you while you get away, then I'll be right behind you." Apparently deciding they'd be able to pick them off soon enough, their pursuers hung back, following close but making no move to engage again.

Diana caught her lower lip between her teeth, glanced out the back window, then back at Emmie. When she seemed to come to the same conclusion he had, that there was no other alternative, she simply nodded and slid closer to the door.

"Ready?"

She blew out a breath. "Yeah."

"On *go*. Three…" He rounded a curve, swerved across the empty oncoming lane, then slammed on the brakes and skidded onto the gravel and dirt shoulder bordering the road. "Two…" Without waiting to come to a full stop, he slammed the shifter into gear. "One…" He shoved the door open and rolled out shooting. "Go, go, go."

FIVE

Diana tucked Emmie against her, covering her head as best she could, and ran. She didn't hesitate, didn't slow down, didn't look back over her shoulder, simply charged as fast as her legs would carry her straight up the incline. Her thigh muscles screamed in protest, ached as she pushed herself even harder. "Please, let me get her out of this. Please, let Chase be okay. Please, help me…help *us*, to protect this child."

The sound of gunfire stalked her, bullets tearing through the brush, and still she ran, dodging trees, bushes, boulders, desperately trying to put some space between her and Emmie and their attackers. Branches slapped against her as she passed, clawing her face, her arms, her hair. She ignored them and kept going.

Emmie hugged her neck in an iron grip.

Silence descended, echoed through Diana's head, rang in her ears. Pinpoints of light danced in front of her eyes, and still, Diana forced herself up the mountainside. The alternative was unacceptable, no matter the cost. But still… Why had it gone so deafeningly quiet? Why had the gunfire stopped? Was Chase okay? He had to be. She wouldn't allow herself to believe anything else.

"Oh, God, please let him be okay," she huffed. No way could she go to Naomi and tell her that her beloved brother hadn't made it. He deserved more time, deserved to know that he'd managed to save this little girl. Not that it would lessen the pain of losing the little boy from eight years ago, but he still needed the victory. And he needed time to return to God, to learn to trust Him again.

Her heart had nearly shattered when he'd chosen to confide in her, understanding how difficult it would have been for him to share his grief, his pain, his guilt. Knowing how impossible it would be for her to do the same. And yet he'd opened up, for just that brief moment, and she'd caught a glimpse of the man he might have been—warm, compassionate, caring.

When Diana had nothing left in her, when her legs threatened to buckle beneath one more step, she dug down and pushed herself harder, grabbing trees and branches to help drag herself up the mountainside as Emmie clung for dear life. She heaved in breath after breath, surged forward, sheer willpower and God's grace the only things keeping her on her feet.

And then he was there. Chase hooked an arm around her waist, supporting some of her weight. He lay a hand against the back of Emmie's head, his own head on a swivel as he urged them forward. "Keep going. It shouldn't be much farther to the rendezvous point."

A sob escaped—just one. Swallowing back the rest of them, Diana nodded and allowed him to guide her as she moved forward, one foot landing in front of the other automatically with no thought for where she was going.

"We're almost there. You've got this." He glanced down into her eyes. "You want me to take her?"

"No." She shook her head, unwilling to relinquish her hold for even a moment, needing the child's weight to push her harder, farther, faster. "I've got it."

"Okay." He kept pace at her side, his arm firm around her, but didn't offer again.

A fact she appreciated, since the pain in her shoulder was just about unbearable, and she might have relented if he'd asked again. But she couldn't. She wouldn't. There was nothing she could do about the people who'd lost their lives because of her eight years ago. Those incredible women had gathered the courage to flee their abusive situations, some of them solely to protect their children, and look where it had gotten them. All because Diana had refused to acknowledge, even to herself, maybe especially to herself, the fact that her own life had veered down that same treacherous, abusive road. If she had, maybe those women, those children—

She cut off the thoughts, had to if she was going to make it up this mountainside. Right now, the past didn't matter. God had entrusted this child to her, and she would keep her safe no matter what. She might not be able to change the past, but she would see to it Emmie didn't suffer the same fate.

Chase chuckled and shook his head. "Thank you, by the way."

"Thank," she wheezed, "you?" She struggled to pull her thoughts from the past. Had she missed something? "For what?"

He hooked a thumb over his shoulder. "For saving my a... Uh..." He glanced at Emmie. "Bacon back there at the cabin."

Diana grinned. She couldn't help it. At least this time

she hadn't had to remind him there was a child present. Seemed maybe there was hope for him yet. "I'm sure you would have done fine on your own."

"No, seriously." His expression sobered. "He might have overpowered me if you hadn't intervened."

"You're welcome, then." Her mind replayed the incident, her shout for him to drop, his instant response. He hadn't hesitated, not even for a second. If he had, the outcome may have been much different. She might have been left to try to fight off both attackers, rescue an unconscious two-hundred-plus-pound man, and see Emmie safe by herself. No way that would have ended well for any of them. "Thank you for trusting me."

He smiled and pulled her closer, nudging her shoulder against him in acknowledgement. "Where'd you learn to fight?"

She shrugged. "I can't fight, really. Naomi taught me a little self-defense."

"Oh, yeah, she mentioned she was teaching a self-defense class at the women's center."

Diana stiffened.

He frowned, obviously noticing, but thankfully didn't ask any questions.

"No, not at the women's center. Just a few private lessons. Number one being…"

"Everything's a weapon," they said together.

This time, she loosened up and laughed. "Yup."

"Well, I'll be sure to let her know her lessons saved us." He started to say something else, but stopped and frowned. "Wait."

A chopper appeared over the next ridge, moving toward them. Stealthy, black, with no markings to identify it.

She nearly fell to her knees and wept with relief, might have if she'd been certain she'd be able to get back up again on her own.

Chase held out an arm to stop her as he pulled out his pistol. He gestured for her to stay put beside a giant pine tree and inched forward, crouched in the shadows at the base of a nearby tree and waited for the pilot to set the chopper down and hop out.

Four people emerged from the chopper—three men and a woman, all dressed in black, all armed with very large, powerful-looking automatic weapons. Between the four of them, it seemed they would be able to cover every conceivable direction a threat could come from.

"Alright." Keeping the weapon in his hand, Chase turned to face her. "This is probably the most dangerous part of the past few hours, but we've got good people with us who are going to do everything they can to keep us safe. The pilot's my boss, Zac Jameson. He's a really good guy and the man I'd trust with this child's safety above all others, except maybe you. So I want you to run straight for the door that agent just opened. Don't hesitate, don't pause, don't look around. You run with Emmie, while Zac's other agents and I cover you. Do you understand?"

She took a deep breath and blew it out slowly, the only outward sign she'd shown of the anxiety plaguing her, and nodded. Then she did exactly as instructed. She tucked Emmie's head against her, covered it and charged uphill in a full-out sprint for the chopper.

Shots erupted from what seemed like every direction as gunmen opened fire and Chase's team responded in kind.

Chase followed closely behind her and Emmie, his movements calm, steady, reassuring amidst the chaos.

A tall handsome woman with sharp, angular features, rich umber skin and closely cropped black hair guided her and Emmie into the chopper, and helped secure them. Her thousand-watt smile belied the fact there were assassins shooting at them. "Hi there, Emmie. I'm Agent Ryan, but you guys can call me Angela. I'm here to help you."

Emmie remained silent as she sank closer against Diana and buried her face against her side.

Angela held out a hand to Diana. "It's a pleasure to meet you. I've read a lot about you."

Diana shook her hand, then wrapped her arm around Emmie.

Chase jumped in beside Zac, who was in the pilot seat, and the other three agents climbed in on either side of Diana and Emmie, bracketing them in safety as they maintained cover fire while Zac lifted off.

The entire scene was surreal. Or maybe the lack of sleep combined with fleeing for their lives and the trek up the mountain had finally caught up with her. Confused, she shook her head and tried to concentrate enough to make sense of the unfolding scene. "How did you read about me?"

"Well, first off, because research is one of my duties at Jameson Investigations, and the first thing Zac had me do when Chase called in was look into your past, present and future." Angela laughed, but a pang of empathy pooled in her intense, dark eyes, then quickly disappeared as she schooled her expression. Obviously, this woman had uncovered way more about her than Diana would have chosen to share.

Diana lowered her gaze.

"And, secondly," Angela continued as if she hadn't just

shattered Diana's illusion of privacy, "Sheriff Adams had some pretty great things to say about you."

Her gaze shot to Angela. "You know Naomi?"

"We met when I was setting up the safe house." She winked, and her grin chased away Diana's fear of the other woman's judgment. "Where she's waiting, not very patiently, I might add, for you all to arrive."

Diana sagged against the seat, pulled Emmie even closer and finally let the tears roll down her cheeks. She'd never been more relieved. Just knowing Naomi was there waiting for her, that she would have already vetted everyone involved in their rescue and pending protection, eased some of the pressure threatening to crush her.

With the immediate threat somewhat removed, she struggled to return her focus to more pressing matters. "Did they clear the rockslide?"

Angela surveyed the landscape. "Not fully, but at least rescue vehicles can squeeze through now on the section of road that wasn't damaged."

The mention of rescue vehicles had Diana sitting up straighter. She should be there, with the rest of her crew, even if the sharp, constant twinge of pain in her shoulder said otherwise. "Was anyone hurt?"

"A couple was reported missing in the area. Not, you know…" She gestured toward Emmie, indicating no one had reported the couple Diana had found. "The missing couple was headed up to a cabin in the mountains for their honeymoon, and no one's heard from them. We can't be sure if they were caught up in the rockslide or if they're safe somewhere, but are simply out of range of a cell tower."

Diana scanned the mountainside and the road winding its way down the mountain beneath them. It only took a few minutes for her to spot a search party. Probably not locals joining with the sheriff's department to hunt for the missing couple, considering the automatic weapons they all carried. She had no illusions the men scouring the mountainside were looking to save anyone. They were looking for her, Chase and Emmie, with the intent to kill. But, at least, they'd stopped shooting for the moment.

One of them pointed toward the chopper.

Another lifted his weapon, but his companion stopped him from firing. Chances were, they couldn't hit the chopper from that distance.

As the man signaled and the group ran back to their vehicles, Diana had no doubt they'd be coming for them as soon as they could regroup.

But why had they entered the cabin stealthily instead of coming in with guns blazing? Were they trying to get to Emmie without the threat of her getting caught in the crossfire? If the group scouring the mountainside was any indication, they certainly had enough men to have easily taken her from them. Perhaps their pursuers hadn't been sure it was them staying in the cabin. Maybe they'd snuck in to check out the situation before calling in reinforcements and launching another attack.

Either way, Diana was just grateful Chase had been awake, and they'd gotten out of there without any further injuries. But what about next time? She cringed as her gaze skipped back to Chase—she was loathe to admit that he was right. They needed help. No way could the two of them keep Emmie safe by themselves. Not without knowing what they were up against, or how such a little girl could warrant the kind of firepower these men toted. They were definitely in way over their heads. At least, she was.

Emmie's weight grew heavier against her side, her breathing deepening into a steady rhythm as she nodded off.

No one had offered Diana a headset, and there was no way to be heard above the sound of the chopper without raising her voice, so she rested her head against the seat back. Her eyes drifted closed. She might not be able to get answers right now, but she would get them the instant they landed. Someone had to have a clue what was so important about this child that an entire group of people were willing to kill to get their hands on her.

Chase stood outside the nondescript, three-bedroom ranch in a small town a few miles outside of Shady Creek and brooded.

Zac Jameson, a tall, solidly built man with a thick cap of salt-and-pepper hair, stood beside him, scanning the narrow residential street. "Something wrong?"

The sun had just begun its ascent, dappling the colorful autumn world in golden light. It was a beautiful small-town scene, reminiscent of a Norman Rockwell painting, if you didn't consider the killers on their heels.

Something was definitely wrong, aside from the obvious. "A feeling in my gut."

Not one to ever dismiss an agent's instincts, Zac stuffed his hands into the pockets of his suit pants and shrugged. "So what's it telling you?"

Zac was also a big believer in talking through things, including your feelings. Most of his agents could attest to the fact that he didn't get very far with that one. They were nothing if not a secretive bunch, though they all stuck together when it mattered. Like now. Chase had answered more than one call for help from Zac and any number of his agents over the years, and now that Chase had called in the cavalry, they'd all responded in kind. And he appreciated it, probably more than they'd ever know. Trust didn't come easy to him, and yet he did trust Zac fully. And he believed in the team Zac had assembled.

So what was bugging him?

Chase scratched his head and pulled a bit of dried leaf from his hair. He needed to get cleaned up and then sleep for about eight hours. Neither of which was likely to happen anytime soon. "They shouldn't have been able to find us."

"No. They shouldn't have," Zac agreed quickly. Too quickly. Which meant he'd already pondered the same issue and come to the same conclusion.

Even though he had complete faith in Zac's team, none of them other than Zac had known Chase's whereabouts, which meant they couldn't possibly have said anything to anyone. "The only people who knew where we were staying, other than Diana and me, were you, Naomi—who would have withstood torture before giving up that little girl's location—and her two deputies…"

Zac nodded and pursed his lips as he glanced over his shoulder at the house his agents currently inhabited. "And Harrison Rhodes."

"Right." The cabin's owner, whom Diana had trusted enough to rely on. "Knowing none of us or Naomi gave anything up can only mean one thing."

"An informant." Ever vigilant, the two men stood at attention on the sidewalk. Zac rocked back on his heels, a gesture that would seem casual to any observer, but actually allowed Chase an unimpeded view of the street behind him.

"Yup." As much as he didn't want to accept that possibility, it had to be seriously considered. "Seems either the sheriff's department or the Shady Creek Fire Department has sprung a leak."

"Exactly."

So now what? They'd have to keep any information on a need-to-know basis. He'd make sure Naomi knew what was happening, but her deputies would have to be left out of the loop for now. As would anyone at the fire department. He just hoped Diana would understand and agree to keep quiet until they could find and plug the leak.

In the meantime, at least he knew he could depend on Zac's team, a fact he should have acknowledged before now.

"Thank you, Zac. Not only for coming to our rescue, but for, well…" He gestured to the house behind him, where all of Zac's vast, almost limitless, resources were hard at work keeping everyone safe while searching for answers. "For everything. I can't tell you how much I appreciate everything you're doing."

Zac put a hand on his shoulder. "I told you when you agreed to join Jameson Investigations that you'd always have a team at your back, and I meant it. Our agents have all suffered through difficult situations, and we all haul around our own heavy baggage, which means sometimes the past comes back to haunt us. But when that happens, we fight it together. You've been around long enough to know that."

Chase nodded, too choked up to say anything more. But he didn't have to.

Zac would understand. He'd suffered his own share of tragedy when his brother, an FBI agent, was killed in a targeted attack. The man's former partner now worked for Jameson Investigations. And, when Zac had gotten the opportunity to take his brother's killer down, Chase had been one of the first agents to respond. "Question is, what do you want to do now?"

Chase shook of his thoughts. "I figured you'd take over the lead on this."

"Nope. I'm here for support and to offer whatever assistance I can, but this investigation is yours." He paused, looked straight through Chase to his very soul. "As long as you want the lead."

Did he? Did he really want to bear the full responsibility for whatever would come next? Did he want more lives on his conscience? It would be so easy to ask Zac to take over, to let him bear the brunt of the decisions and their consequences. And Zac would do it in a heartbeat, with no questions asked, and he'd never judge Chase for being a coward.

But Chase would know the truth. He shook Zac's hand. "Thanks."

"Anytime."

"So what's next?" he said, mostly to himself. Plan after plan ran through his mind, as he rapidly dismissed each one. The most important thing was to keep Diana and Emmie safe, but without understanding what was behind the threat, that was easier said than done. Which led to their current problem—they had no idea who was after them or why. They needed more information, but without further clues, he didn't know where to start. Plus, there was the issue of who might have leaked their whereabouts. If he was being honest with himself, that was the most pressing problem, and the one he was looking least forward to dealing with.

Zac glanced back at the house. "I think you already know."

"Yeah, I suppose I do." Although he dreaded the thought

of facing both Diana and Naomi and telling them that someone they trusted had most likely betrayed them.

"Of course…" Zac shrugged. "There's always the possibility your two attackers found the cabin by chance, noticed the lights on, then decided to stop in and check out who might be staying in the cabin."

While he appreciated the out, he was already shaking his head. "They had too many men all over the area, including those lying in wait to pursue us the instant we left the driveway. It was too coordinated to have been an accident. No way they just happened upon us. They knew right where we'd be."

"I agree."

The front door opened, and Angela strolled out, paused to tilt her face up to the sun, then resumed her trek. She flashed her killer smile when she reached them. "Hey, guys. You might want to come inside."

Chase stiffened. They'd found something. The three of them sauntered back inside, careful to appear ordinary and casual to any observers. No sense drawing attention to themselves. For the safe house to be effective, they had to blend in.

The instant Chase crossed the threshold, his gaze slid down the hallway to where Diana sat, chewing a thumbnail, on a chair outside a closed door behind which Dr. Rogers, a gentle man with a robust personality and a perpetually calm demeanor, tended to Emmie. While Chase didn't know much about his history, he did know Dr. Rogers had been with Zac since he'd first founded Jameson Investigations, and he'd saved more than one of their miserable hides.

He turned his attention from Diana, and his thoughts from Emmie and Dr. Rogers, to survey the living room.

Computers had been set up throughout the room, along with printers, copiers and an assortment of surveillance equipment. The hastily assembled office could function as well as any command center.

Angela slid onto a seat next to Naomi.

Chase leaned over and kissed his sister's head. "Hey, sis."

"Hey." She gripped the hand he'd placed on her shoulder. "Sorry about all this."

"Are you kidding me? This is the best vacation I've had in years."

"Yeah, right." She swiveled the chair to face him, then gestured around the room. "Seriously, Chase. Thank you for all of this. I couldn't bear it if…"

"Hey." Ignoring everyone else in the room, he crouched in front of her, took her hand in his. "Nothing is going to happen to that little girl. Or to Diana."

Tears shimmered in her eyes, darkening her lashes, then finally tipped over. She nodded, sniffed.

"Look at me, Naomi." He lifted her chin until she had no choice but to look into his eyes. *I won't let anything happen to them.* He wanted to utter the words so badly, to reassure her, comfort her, but they stuck in his throat, and he choked on them.

She shook her head and lowered her gaze, guilt clearly eating at her. "I should have insisted the woman stay with me when she first told me she and her daughter were in danger. I should have followed her, should have offered her protection."

"With only you and two deputies?" He wouldn't allow her to shoulder the blame for this. "Look, Naomi. The woman could have stayed and told you more about what was going on. She chose not to. When she asked you to meet her, you agreed. There wasn't anything more you could have done."

"I guess. But it doesn't help me feel any better about how things turned out."

"Maybe not, but all you can do for her now is protect her child, and you *are* doing that."

She nodded, seeming less than reassured.

But there was nothing he could say to convince her, so, instead, he patted her hand, stood and turned to Angela. "So what's up? Did you find something?"

"Naomi worked with a sketch artist Zac brought in to get a picture of the woman."

"Barry Grant?"

She nodded absently as she rifled through a stack of pages.

"He's good."

"The best," she agreed and started typing rapidly while reading a report at the same time. Angela took multitasking to a whole new level. No wonder Jameson Investigations was so dependent on her.

An image popped up on the screen, pulling his attention from the agent. It showed a woman in her late twenties or early thirties, with long, shaggy dark hair. Her dark eyes seemed lifeless, but whether that was the way Naomi remembered her or just the way they appeared in the black-and-white sketch, he didn't know. A profile sketch showed an ivy tattoo running from behind her left ear, down her neck, just as Diana had described at the hospital.

"Do you have an ID?"

"Not yet, but Naomi's going through mug shots, and we're using facial-recognition software, so hopefully..."

"You think she's been arrested before?"

Naomi shrugged. "She said her husband was into something illegal, and she wouldn't stay and talk to me anywhere near the station, so I just figured, maybe…"

He nodded. They were essentially searching for a needle in a haystack.

"We know she was from New York City, so that at least narrows it down some." The look she sent him was anything but hopeful.

A door opened down the hallway, and Dr. Rogers stepped out.

"Excuse me for a minute. I'll be right back." Chase hurried toward where the doctor was talking to Diana, who'd stood when he'd emerged from the room. Her injured arm was in a sling and held tightly against her body.

Chase squeezed her uninjured arm in support, a friendly gesture to let her know she wasn't alone, as she'd done for him when he'd needed someone. Then he stuffed his hands into his pockets and leaned his back against the wall next to her.

Dr. Rogers continued speaking, his voice gruff, his blue eyes somber. "…sustained the kind of injuries you'd expect between the fire, the explosion and then going on the run through the woods. Nothing serious. And, thankfully, her arm's not broken."

"What about past injuries?" The bruises on her arm still bothered him. They'd assumed the killer had put them there, but there was always the possibility it had been someone closer to her.

"You're referring to the bruises around her upper arm?" the doctor asked.

"Yes. We suspected they were finger marks, but…" He didn't need to spell it out.

"I agree." He wrapped his hand around Chase's arm in the same spot the bruises had appeared on Emmie. "If someone grabbed her here and squeezed, it would leave marks just like that. But, it seems to me whoever it was pulled her toward them and held her, squeezing for more than the quick second it would have taken to, say, grab hold and fling her away."

"Did you find any other signs of abuse?"

He was already shaking his head. "If I had to guess, I'd say the bruising happened sometime last night, probably right before the fire. And there are no other signs she's been abused. She's a little small for her age, but well nourished, no sign of past injuries, no scarring. Though she is timid and frightened, that's to be expected, considering the ordeal she's been through over the past couple of days."

"Who's with her now?" Because Chase had no doubt he wouldn't have left her unsupervised.

"Shae Payne."

Relief rushed through him. If anyone knew how to deal with a traumatized child, it was Shae. "Is Mason here?"

The doctor hooked his thumb down the hallway toward the back of the house. "He came straight from an assignment and hadn't slept in thirty-six hours. Zac wouldn't let him near anything until he took a six-hour power nap."

Chase grinned. "He's such a mother hen."

Dr. Rogers laughed, a deep, full-on belly laugh that could ease the tension from the most intense of situations. "That he is. But, you know Mason. He'd have jumped right in with no rest at all if Zac hadn't forced him to take some downtime. To be honest—" he winked at Diana "—if I poked my head in that room right now, I'd probably find him on his cell phone or laptop searching for information instead of napping."

"You're probably right." But his presence brought Chase a certain amount of reassurance. He'd worked with Mason Payne before, and he was a good man, as well as a great agent. The kind of man you'd want to have your back under the circumstances.

"Is it okay if I go in and see Emmie now?" Diana asked.

"Sure thing. Just don't push her too much right now. She needs some rest, and she needs to feel safe. She'll open up when she's ready and when she figures out who she can trust."

"Thank you, Doctor. And thank you for taking care of my injuries." She held a hand out to him.

"Of course, dear. Anytime." He shook her proffered hand, patted her arm and smiled. "I'll be back in to check on you both in a little while."

Diana opened the bedroom door, and Chase started to follow her inside.

"Hey, Chase, hold up a sec." Angela hurried toward him, a folder in her hand.

"Go ahead, Diana. I'll check in after I'm done." He peeked in the doorway to see Emmie sitting cross-legged on the bed coloring, with Shae keeping watch from an armchair a few feet away, then closed the door behind Diana. "What's up, Angela?"

Angela held out the folder. "We just ID'd the guy from the fire."

SIX

Grateful to be off her feet, Diana perched on the edge of the armchair next to Shae's. They'd met only briefly after Dr. Rogers had tended to Diana's injuries and before Shae and Dr. Rogers had hurried inside the bedroom-turned-infirmary with Emmie and closed the door behind them. "How's she doing?"

Shae set aside the book she'd been holding open and pretending to read while she watched Emmie like a hawk. The fact that it was upside down was a pretty big hint as to what was really holding her attention. "She's okay. She's not talking, but she's making that beautiful picture."

Emmie didn't acknowledge her presence, simply continued to color. She'd changed into pajamas and slippers Zac's agents must have provided and looked so tiny and vulnerable on the queen-size bed.

Diana studied the picture, a mass of different colored scribbles she couldn't make sense out of. Seemed there was a lot of that going around lately—things she couldn't make sense of. Like, why had Chase opened up to her about his past? He'd said he felt bad about not carrying Emmie for her. He couldn't possibly realize Emmie was no burden to her, but a chance to maybe save one child when she hadn't been able to save others. Of course, if she'd been able to find the same courage he had, and explain to him about her own past, maybe he would understand. Would she ever tell him? Would she ever tell anyone? About the abuse she'd suffered at the hands of the man who should have loved her? Worse, about the people he'd killed because of her? She shied away from the thoughts, had to if she were going to keep control of her emotions.

None of that mattered now. It couldn't. What mattered was keeping Emmie safe—and Chase was the one who had made that possible. Whether or not Diana would ever trust another man completely, Chase had proven himself, over and over again, as he'd risked his life to save not just Emmie, but Diana, too. He'd earned her respect. And her trust…as far as this situation was concerned, anyway.

Emmie seemed to know what she was drawing, as she focused intently on her task, chewing on her lower lip with a way-too-grown-up scowl firmly in place.

Not wanting to interrupt, Diana checked the urge to reach out and wrap an arm around her.

"The counsel, uh…" Shae paused, seemed to consider her words. "A woman is coming to help us out here. She's a friend of mine, and she's very nice, one of the best people Zac knows, but she was on another assignment across the country and couldn't get here until later tonight or early tomorrow morning."

Diana nodded, relief rushing through her. First and foremost, Emmie needed someone who actually knew how to care for her. Plus, as much as she hated to admit it, they needed someone who could get Emmie to open up and give them some information. They had nothing to go on, no clues to the identity of the victims, no idea who Emmie was or where she came from. Even the smallest lead might help them figure out who was trying to hurt her. Because, not only was it clear there was more than one person involved, but it was also apparent they were never going to give up. Whoever was after this little girl commanded resources. Which meant, even if they managed to apprehend one attacker, there would likely be others to take his place. No, they had to get to the root of this problem. And the only leads they might have were locked up in that child's head.

Diana eased herself against the seatback as gently as possible, every injury begging her to move slowly. She rested her head, eyes slitted to keep watch over Emmie.

"You okay?" Shae asked.

"Yes, thank you." She tilted her head toward Shae without lifting it. She'd almost forgotten the other woman was there. "Just exhausted."

Shae reached out to her, gripped her hand. "I understand exactly how you feel, and if you need someone to talk to, I'm here for you. I understand what you're going through."

Diana scooted up a little straighter. "You've been through something similar?"

She nodded, pain filling her eyes. "Yes, with my daughter."

"Did she…? Were you…? I mean…" As much as she wanted to know the outcome, she couldn't force the words out, couldn't bear to find out they'd failed.

Shae smiled and lay a hand on her belly, and the baby growing within. "Gracie's fine and very excited to meet her new little brother or sister. Not that there aren't lingering issues, but Maddy Hunter has helped a lot."

"Is that the woman who's coming for…?" She gestured toward Emmie.

"It is, yes."

"That's good." She felt better knowing the therapist had a proven track record, though she didn't doubt that anyone Jameson Investigations brought in would be capable, considering Zac Jameson seemed more than competent. She'd learned to trust her fellow firefighters, even after everything that had happened with Liam, so if she viewed Zac as a working relationship, maybe she could learn to trust him, too. She owed it to Chase to at least try.

Emmie lifted her head, interrupting any further conversation. She held up the scribble drawing, which consisted of mostly red and black. Tears tracked down her already raw cheeks as she held it out to Diana.

Ignoring the stabbing pains throughout her body, Diana shifted onto the edge of the bed and held out her hand. "Is that for me?"

Emmie glanced at Shae from the corners of her eyes, then cast her gaze downward.

"You know what?" Shae stood. "I think I'm going to go make some hot chocolate. Would either of you like some?"

"Sure." Diana smiled, kept her posture relaxed. "That would be nice. Right, Emmie?"

Without lifting her gaze, Emmie nodded.

"I'll be back in a little bit." She held Diana's gaze for a moment, raising her eyebrows in a silent reminder of what Dr. Rogers had told her when he'd first come out of the bedroom after examining Emmie. *If she decides to open up, let her take the lead. Don't coax her or try to pry information from her, simply let her guide the conversation.*

"Got it. Thank you."

"Of course." Shae left, closing the door quietly behind her.

Emmie curled against Diana's side and stuck her thumb

in her mouth. At three years old, should she still be sucking her thumb? Or had she reverted to a comforting habit from when she was younger?

Diana had no idea and wished fervently that the counselor was there to guide her through this new territory.

She held Emmie's paper and turned so the two of them could view it together. She draped one arm loosely over Emmie, trying to offer comfort without making her feel trapped. "So what do we have here?"

Emmie pointed to a pink blob and said around her thumb, "Mommy."

"This is your mommy?"

She nodded against Diana's side.

Great. Now what? She wished there was someone else there to help her navigate this, but until the counselor arrived, they were giving Emmie space to choose whom she would trust. And it seemed she may have chosen to place that trust in Diana. *God, please guide me. Please, help me know what to do for this little girl. Please, don't let me fail her.*

She took a deep, shaky breath and blew it out slowly. "Can you tell me Mommy's name?"

She rubbed her fingers over the pink crayon spot. "Mommy."

Right.

Then she slid her finger across the page and traced an angry slash of black. "Bad man."

Everything in Diana went still. "That is the bad man?"

Emmie nodded again.

Okay. She could do this. Dr. Rogers had said not to lead her. So she'd have to be very careful how she phrased any questions. She closed her eyes and inhaled deeply, searching for guidance. "Why is the man bad?"

"Made Mommy have boo-boos." She rubbed her arm. "Made me a boo-boo."

Diana's heart squeezed painfully in her chest. Suddenly, it seemed more important to ease Emmie's fears than it did to find answers. "The bad man can't hurt you anymore."

Emmie popped her thumb back into her mouth.

Diana shifted the little girl into her lap and looked her in the eye. "I promise, I won't let the bad man hurt you anymore. There are a lot of people here to make sure that doesn't happen. Me, and Chase, and Zac, and Shae. And all of the other people here are going to protect you. Do you understand? You are safe now."

She knew better than to make that promise, but her heart just wouldn't allow her to accept any other outcome, wouldn't allow her to leave this child afraid and uncertain.

Emmie's eyes started to drift closed.

"Emmie?"

They popped back open.

"Do you know the bad man's name?"

She studied Diana for a long moment, the seconds ticking by in slow motion as Diana held her breath until Emmie nodded. Then, without another word, she closed her eyes and curled up in Diana's arms.

Accepting she wasn't going to say anything more, Diana simply sat with Emmie, rocking her gently back and forth, humming softly until the girl's breathing slowed to a steady rhythm. Then she rocked her a little longer. Finally, when she was absolutely certain Emmie was really asleep, and not just playing possum, she lay her on the bed and covered her with a blanket. She stood over her for another moment, silently vowing to keep her safe, then headed for the door.

Leaving it open behind her, in case Emmie became

frightened and cried out, Diana strode into the living room and utter chaos.

Several agents spoke at once, some pointing things out on maps or computer screens, others flipping through stacks of papers. She sought out Chase and found him and Zac hunched over either side of Angela's seat, staring at a computer screen.

Shae intercepted her and handed her a mug of hot chocolate. "Is she asleep?"

"Yes."

"That's probably best. I'll sit with her while you get caught up here."

Diana nodded her appreciation. "She said she knows who killed her mother."

The entire room went dead silent, the lack of sound almost deafening.

Chase was the first to shoot to his feet and move toward Diana, with Zac close on his heels.

Her cheeks heated. "I'm sorry. I didn't mean… She didn't tell me who it was. I didn't mean to get everyone's hopes up."

"That's okay. Don't worry about it. Maddy will probably be able to coax more information from her tomorrow." Chase wrapped his hand around hers holding the mug. "Drink this. Your hands are like ice."

"There are fresh clothes in the back bedroom if you want to get cleaned up and changed." Shae excused herself to go sit with Emmie, and Chase stepped back and shoved his hands into his pockets.

Zac folded his arms across his chest. "What did she say?"

"She drew a picture. She pointed out her mom and what she called a bad man. She said he hurt both her mother and her." Diana inhaled the rich sweet scent of cocoa and took a sip. Warmth rushed through her, chasing away the chill she had been afraid might be permanent. "Then I asked her if she knew the bad man's name, and she nodded. Of course, when I asked if she knew her mother's name, she said Mommy, so it's possible you wouldn't be able to get an ID from her even if she did share it."

Zac patted her arm. "Shae will stay with her. Why don't you do as she suggested and get cleaned up, then get some sleep in case she needs you again."

Diana nodded. "Thank you."

When he walked away, Chase led her to a couch against the far wall and gestured for her to sit. Instead of sitting next to her, he sat on the coffee table facing her.

Her stomach burned, and she set the hot chocolate on the side table. "I'm sorry I couldn't get anything more from her. Dr. Rogers said—"

"Hey." He gripped her hands. His touch was warm, strong, a lifeline amid utter uncertainty. "You did great. That's more than we expected her to say."

"But it doesn't help anything."

"Actually, it does."

She looked up, searching for the truth in his eyes.

"Once we can ID the mother, we'll be able to search for known associates. If Emmie knows him, he had to have been involved with her mother in some way, close enough that she'd have brought him around her three-year-old daughter. If nothing else, maybe we can show Emmie pictures of potential suspects."

"I suppose." Though the idea of Emmie sifting through mug shots in search of her attacker didn't sit well. She started to speak her mind, then bit her tongue. Why bother?

That argument could wait for another time, if it even became necessary. The more pressing issue was how to get Emmie to give them the bad man's name. But would she really have anything useful to say?

Even if the killer was her father, she might only know him as Daddy. How could they identify him from that? And, who was the man Diana had found in the cabin with Emmie's mother? A dull throb started at her temples.

Chase released her hands, sat back and clasped his hands between his knees. "Okay, there are two things you need to know."

She lifted an eyebrow and waited, relieved he was including her in whatever was going on. The thought he might freeze her out now that he had his team backing him had lingered for the past few hours, probably contributing to her headache.

"First, the couple that was lost in the rockslide has been located."

She held her breath.

"They're fine. Alive and well. They were just out of range for a while, and they are now safe, accounted for and continuing to enjoy their honeymoon."

She blew the breath out slowly, grateful Chase had realized it would bother her if she didn't know what had happened to them. "That's great, Chase. Thank you for letting me know."

"Sure thing." He smiled, creasing the dimple in his cheek, and held his hand out to her. "We're in this together, right?"

She laughed and shook her head but gave the offered hand a hard pump. "You bet."

When he pulled his hand back and his expression sobered, she found herself wishing they could just back up one moment, and he would continue to offer her that incredible smile he so rarely indulged in…at least, since she'd met him. Of course, they'd been on the run from a pack of clearly organized assassins for all of that time, but still…

"The second thing is, we identified the male victim from the fire."

"Is that what was going on when I walked out?"

"Yes."

"How? Who is he? Do you know if he's Emmie's father? What about the woman? Have you figured out who she was?" She struggled to switch gears from the lighthearted moment they'd just shared to the buzz of excitement at a potential lead. For some reason, Chase seemed to possess a natural talent for keeping her off balance.

"Whoa, slow down." He frowned and sat up straighter, then scratched his head, tousling his thick blond-streaked hair. "That's the thing. We don't know yet if he's her father, or even if he's connected to her in any way, and we may not figure that out until we can identify the mother. We got the positive ID on him because his fingerprints were all over the SUV found in front of the cabin and the wallet with the forged ID. They were on record because he's a PI, but the woman either wasn't in the SUV to leave prints, or her prints aren't in the system.

"As far as being Emmie's father—there's no record of him being married or fathering a child, but that doesn't rule him out. What we do know, is that he is, or was, a private investigator from New York City."

She had no idea what she'd been expecting. A mob boss? A drug runner? Even a gang member. But a PI was nowhere on her list. "If he's not Emmie's father, do you think he was involved with her mother in some way? Dating, maybe? Or could she have been a client?"

"We have no idea yet, and there's only one way to find out."

"What's that?"

"I have to go into the city. I'll be taking Zac's chopper first thing in the morning and going to the private investigator's office."

Her heart raced. For the first time, they might be on track to getting answers. Then reality hit her like a sucker punch as she realized that she'd probably be left out of the loop, only hearing about whatever they found after the fact.

"Maddy Hunter is already on her way, and she'll spend most of the day with Emmie. Plus, Shae will be here, and Dr. Rogers." He hesitated, seemed reluctant to say anything more. "So if you want… You don't have to… I just thought… Maybe, if you want…"

"You said that already." She couldn't help but grin. "And, yes. In answer to the question I think you're stumbling through, I would like to accompany you to New York City tomorrow morning."

As much as she hated to leave Emmie, she couldn't bear the thought of sitting around the safe house all day long doing nothing while the doctors took care of Emmie. She couldn't do anything for her here. The best she could do to help her would be to find answers.

Chase was lying in the dark, his head propped on one arm of the couch, his feet on the other, beating himself up over asking Diana if she wanted to go to the city with him. He hadn't intended to ask. Why would he, when he had an entire team of experts dedicated to seeking the truth who could back him up?

And then her expression had fallen, and she'd seemed so crushed at the thought of the investigation moving on without her. But why not take her? She'd been with the investigation since the beginning, had proven herself strong and courageous and smart. Actually, if not for her bravery in the first place, running into that burning cabin, Emmie would no doubt be long gone. Diana deserved a chance to see this through. And Zac had agreed.

Chase swung his feet over the side of the couch someone had moved into one of the bedrooms and sat up. Apparently, two hours was as much sleep as he was going to get. He sighed and scrubbed his hands over his face. No sense lying there wasting time. He'd get up, eat something and go over the notes Angela had compiled on the murdered PI. Who knew? Maybe something would jump out at him that the others had missed. He doubted it, but it couldn't hurt to—

A scream had him on his feet, gun in hand. He flew through the door before the echo finished reverberating.

As he reached Emmie's door, it whipped open, and Shae stood in the doorway holding up her hands to block the dozen or so agents all crammed into the hallway with their weapons drawn. "It's all right. Just a nightmare."

The other agents dispersed. All except Shae's husband, Mason. He slung an arm around his wife and pulled her close. Knowing what the two of them had been through last Christmas, Chase couldn't blame him. Emmie's scream must have nearly stopped his heart.

Chase holstered his weapon. "That poor kid."

Shae pursed her lips and glanced over her shoulder, then shook her head. "Not Emmie."

His heart stuttered. Maybe he'd been wrong. Maybe he shouldn't have involved Diana any further in this investigation. Maybe he was asking too much of her. "Is she okay?"

"Yeah, just a nightmare. But it must have been a bad one."

"Do you think she'd talk to me for a minute?" For what? Was he hoping to help her in some way? Fat chance of that happening, considering he was probably more of a mess than she was. He was damaged beyond repair, and he had no idea how to heal himself, much less anyone else. But she'd been a friend to him in a moment of weakness. The least he could do was return the favor.

"I think she could probably use a friend right now." Shae smiled and stepped aside for him to enter, then wrapped her arm around Mason's waist and rested her head against his shoulder as the two of them wandered toward the kitchen.

Chase turned away, knowing that level of love and commitment wasn't meant for him anymore, not after he'd let his wife down. He'd never again be able to open up enough to someone, to lower his guard and let someone close enough to share his life. Not when he was so convinced he'd just let them down, too. And for the first time, the reality saddened him.

He turned away and knocked softly on the open door. "Can I come in?"

"Yes," Diana answered softly, her voice lacking its usual fortitude.

He eased the door the rest of the way open, the light from the hallway spilling over Emmie, who appeared asleep, still curled on the bed beneath a blanket. Chase couldn't tell if she'd somehow slept through the scream, had gone back to

sleep afterward, or was just feigning sleep, which seemed
to be her go-to escape mechanism.

Diana sat upright in the armchair, her feet propped on
the bottom corner of the footboard. She pulled her sweat-
shirt sleeves down over her hands, then tucked them beneath her chin. "I'm sorry I woke you."

Leaving the door open, he moved to sit in the empty
armchair beside her. "Don't worry about it. I was already
up. I don't sleep much."

If the haunted look on her face and the dark, puffy rings
circling her eyes were any indication, neither did she. She
lay her head against the chair back and closed her eyes.

"You want to talk about it?"

She shrugged. "Not really."

"I can certainly understand that. But speaking as someone who recently spilled my guts to a friend, I can tell you
it helps to have someone to talk to." The truth of that statement caught him off guard. It *had* helped to talk to her, had
alleviated some of his guilt at letting her bear the burden of
always carrying Emmie, but he hadn't realized that until
just this moment, watching her hands shake as she exposed
them for a moment to push her hair behind her ears.

She smiled then. It didn't reach her eyes, but at least
she'd made the attempt.

"Okay, then, if you don't want to talk, how about you try
to get a few more hours sleep? I'll sit right in the doorway
to make sure no one comes near you or Emmie." Because
he had a sneaking suspicion it wasn't her own safety she
was concerned for.

"No, it's okay."

"All right." He started to stand. "Sorry to bother you."

"No. Wait. I'm sorry." She shook her head, brushed her

hair back again when it tumbled into her eyes. "I'd like you to sit with me, please. It's just…"

He resumed sitting, watching Emmie breathe softly while he waited for Diana to figure out what she wanted to say. He'd just sit with her, keep her company, ease her fears if he could.

"My nightmares aren't from this…" She waved a hand around the room, gestured toward the hive of activity going on just outside the door, even this late into the night. She took a deep breath, like a diver about to plunge headfirst off a cliff, and turned to face him. "I was engaged once."

It didn't surprise him. She was a kind woman—caring, compassionate, supportive, strong, always seemed to put others first. And beautiful, too. Of course, she'd have her pick of men wanting to marry her. What did surprise him was the pain in her expression. Whatever tragedy had ended her engagement, she'd clearly never gotten over it.

"To make a long, horrible story short, he was abusive, controlling and an all-around…" She glanced at Emmie then released some of the pent-up tension, relaxing her posture. The child seemed to have a calming effect on her, no matter how dire the circumstances. "Somehow, even while volunteering at a shelter for abused women and children, I missed all the signs that my own relationship wasn't very different from theirs."

"Sometimes, it's more difficult to see what's right in front of you. As an outsider looking in, I think you get a clearer view."

"Thank you for saying that, but I still should have realized what he was doing. I made it too easy for him to manipulate me. I was too eager to please him, to make him happy, to put his needs ahead of everyone else's." Tears tracked down her cheeks, reflecting brilliantly in the hall-way light, and she swiped them away with her sleeves. "The only thing I refused to give up, no matter how he ca-joled or begged or whined or demanded, was my work at the shelter. So..."

Her voice hitched.

He curled his hands into fists, wishing, however briefly, he could use them on her former fiancé.

"One night..." She lowered her voice to a near whisper, and he had to lean forward to hear her. "He burned it down."

Chase felt like he'd been slapped in the face. He had to have heard her wrong. "He did what?"

She nodded, sniffed. Her voice turned raspy, hoarse, as she strained to finish this. "With everyone inside—the women I'd tried to help, the children that had given their mothers the courage to walk out on their abusers... Every-one. He was a firefighter. He was supposed to save people. Instead, he barred the doors, used an accelerant. It went up in the middle of the night and was fully engulfed before the firefighters even got there."

And yet, she'd gone into that cabin certain she smelled an accelerant. The reminder must have tortured her the en-tire time. And then to find—

He shoved to his feet, crossed the room and grabbed a box of tissues from the nightstand. Working to get his emo-tions under control, he returned and handed her the box, then turned his chair to face hers. He sat, taking both of her hands in his. "It wasn't your fault. You know that, right?"

She shrugged and averted her gaze. "That's what the counselor said. But if I'd recognized him for the monster he was sooner, those women and children might all still be alive."

"And they might not be." He squeezed her hands to bring her attention back to him. "I understand how you feel, Diana."

"You don't understand. You can't." Her face twisted into a pained expression, and she yanked her hands from his, shoved them into her hair and squeezed. "I was supposed to be there that night. I told him I was going. We had a terrible fight because he wanted me to go with him to some stuffy function, and I said I'd already committed to spending the evening at the shelter. And then…"

She paused, sucked in a deep, shaky breath and dropped her hands into her lap. "He slapped me, hard, across the face."

Chase clenched his fists, wishing he could get his hands on that guy for one minute, then forced himself to relax and sit back. His rage would do nothing to ease her suffering, might only fuel her pain.

She pulled her hands back into her sleeves and wrapped her arms around herself, then rocked back and forth. "I stormed out of the house, but how could I show up at the shelter with a handprint across my face? How could I explain that? I'd talked with so many women who worried that they'd made a mistake coming to the shelter. They'd been gaslit into believing that they deserved to be hit and verbally abused, that they had to stay with their abusive husband or boyfriend because they'd never be able to get by without them. I worked hard every day to help them see that walking away had been the right choice—that they deserved better than the treatment they'd gotten. How could I expect them to listen to a word I said when they could see that I'd fallen into the same trap? I couldn't handle the thought of it, so instead, I went and sat by the lake. I sat there, with no clue what to do, while all of those people died because of me. How can I live with that? It should have been me."

"If it should have been you, it would have been."

"But why would God spare me? Why would He, when it was all my fault?"

"First of all, it wasn't your fault. And second, I can't speak to God's plans. On that score, I'm lost myself. But I do know, if He spared you, there was a reason. Did you ever think maybe it was for this moment, so you'd be here to save this child?" He gestured toward Emmie, finally sleeping peacefully. "I know what it's like to carry that guilt, to live knowing you might have saved lives had you done things differently, but we only get one chance, Diana." He knew that better than anyone. "Sometimes all we can do is move forward, one day at a time, one minute at a time, and try to do better."

"Is that how you get through the days?"

"Some." He nodded.

"And others?"

"Other days, I torture myself with what life might be like had I done something, anything, differently."

She squeezed her eyes closed tight, dabbed at them with the tissue and opened them again. She stared at him, her eyes filled with a question he knew she needed an answer to. "Could you have? If you'd done something differently, would it have saved your wife and that little boy?"

He shook his head. He'd gone over every second of that night more times than he could count—the pain of the bullet that took him down, the agony of watching his wife bleed out without even being able to get to her, to hold her in his arms so she wouldn't die alone, dragging himself across the pavement in a desperate attempt to reach Connor. The instant he knew he wouldn't make it, followed by the horror of watching the little boy fall and the life drain from his eyes. Knowing he would have to tell Naomi he'd failed to protect her—

The darkest moment of his life.

"Not in that moment, no. I couldn't have changed how things went that night." He did know that, no matter how difficult it had been to accept. "But before that. I trusted people I shouldn't have, and it eventually led to that outcome. So I do understand what you're going through. And I'm here for you. If you need a friend to sit with you, a hand to hold, a shoulder to cry on, or a target to vent your frustrations all over, I'm your guy."

"Thank you." She tried to give him a smile, but it was more like a grimace of pain. "I appreciate that. And you're right about one thing."

He lifted an eyebrow. "Only one?"

That elicited a more genuine smirk. "I do feel a little... lighter, I guess, after saying all of that. If that makes sense?"

"It makes perfect sense." He stood and held a hand out to her.

"Thank you." She took his hand and allowed him to help her up. "I haven't talked about that night in so long, I think it was eating away at me more than I even realized. Once I stopped going to therapy, I just kept it all bottled up inside."

"Yeah, I get it." He reached out and tipped up her chin so she'd have no choice but to meet his gaze, just like she'd done for him when he'd tried so hard to avoid the truth. "Why don't we both promise each other we'll try not to do that anymore."

Her gaze lingered on his eyes. If she was searching for judgment there, she wouldn't find it. "Okay."

"If something's bothering you, just reach out."

"And vice versa."

He slid his hand into her hair, smoothed it back behind her ear as he'd seen her do so many times, then dropped it to his side. The last thing he wanted to do was send the wrong impression. She needed a friend, and maybe he did, too, but he wouldn't want her to think it could ever be anything more than friendship.

He'd let down his wife, his sister, her son... Naomi would live in pain for the rest of her life because he hadn't protected her child when he'd promised he would. After failing so miserably, how could he possibly deserve happiness? How could he deserve love? And, if he did ever open up and allow himself to love again, what if he failed her just as badly? That just wasn't a chance he could take. "Why don't we get some breakfast and head out. If neither of us is going to sleep, anyway, we may as well make use of the time."

"Okay, hang on." She turned away, took another blanket from the foot of the bed and tucked it around Emmie.

She whimpered but didn't wake.

Chase turned, paused for a moment to reflect on what might have been, then bottled all of those emotions back up and started out the door. They needed to get to New York, and there was no time to waste. The sooner they got the victims identified, the sooner they could figure out who wanted to kill Diana and snatch Emmie, and the sooner he could return to his life of solitude, trusting no one but the man who'd saved him from himself all those years ago. And maybe Diana.

"Chase. Hold up," Diana called from the foot of the bed.

He walked back to her. "What's up? She okay?"

"I… I'm not sure what your beliefs are, but I was wondering, if you wouldn't mind, um…" She wrung her hands together. "Would you mind praying with me before we leave?"

She looked so fragile in that moment, worried, scared and unsure what his reaction would be. He walked over and took her hands in his.

"I'd be happy to." And it surprised him to realize, the idea brought a sense of peace. Seemed he was learning an awful lot about himself from Diana Cameron.

SEVEN

Revealing a part of herself she'd kept hidden for so long had left Diana drained. She looked out over the landscape as the chopper banked and the New York City skyline, set ablaze by the first rays of the morning sun, came into view. She sat up straighter in the seat, awed by the view, despite the dire circumstances of their visit.

Chase grinned. "Incredible, isn't it?"

"It really is."

"Have you ever seen New York from a helicopter?"

"Actually, I've never been to New York City before. I researched a number of areas from Florida before I left, and when the job in Shady Creek became available, I took it and drove up with all my stuff in an SUV." She'd left Florida with nothing more than a few new outfits she'd picked up and the locket her mother had given her for her sixteenth birthday. Everything else, she'd donated to charity. She wanted nothing to remind herself of that time in her new home. Instead, she'd filled her cabin with cozy, rustic furniture she'd picked up from local craftsman one piece at a time over the past four years.

She shifted to look out the side window at the harbor

and the Statue of Liberty. "It's so much bigger than it looks in pictures."

"Yes, it is." Chase pointed out the window. "If you look over there, you can see the Freedom Tower."

She followed his directions, amazed by the towering skyscrapers and the sheer number of buildings crammed into one space.

He started to descend, and she gripped her seat and then laughed. At first, having Chase behind the controls had scared her to death. For some reason, she'd assumed there'd be a pilot. But he seemed to know what he was doing, so she left him to it and continued to enjoy the view. She'd love the chance to return one day when there wasn't so much at stake.

Leaving Emmie behind had been more difficult than she'd anticipated. She'd become more attached to the little girl than she was willing to admit, even to herself—maybe especially to herself. Even after Shae had assured her that she and Mason would protect her, Diana had almost backed out and told Chase to take Zac with him instead. Except, she had a feeling that would have been more cowardice than anything else. What Emmie needed from her now was in an office in New York City. She hoped, anyway.

Diana held her breath, her heart in her throat, along with her stomach, as Chase aimed for a rooftop that appeared no bigger than a kid's trampoline. "Are you sure we're going to fit on there?"

He laughed and banked to the side. "It's bigger than it looks."

"I sure hope so." It seemed so natural to laugh with him. She found she actually liked this more easygoing version of Chase. But even the brooding, serious attitude he usually projected didn't bother her as much now as it had at first. Maybe now that she'd taken the time to get to know him, to understand his suffering, his personality made more sense to her. She swallowed the lump in her throat that was threatening to choke her. Tears pricked the backs of her lids, and she closed her eyes to keep them contained.

"You okay?"

"What? Oh, yeah. I'm good." She still couldn't believe she'd told him about her past, that she'd even talked about it at all. But she did feel better, as if she didn't bear the burden alone now. If her mind wandered down that dark road again, she wouldn't be as afraid to open up to him about her thoughts and feelings.

A small bump pulled her back to the present, and when she opened her eyes, they were on the roof surrounded by the most incredible view. "Why did we land on a roof, anyway?"

"With the resources our pursuers seem to have at their disposal, we were concerned they'd have the Heliport watched."

She nodded, leaving Chase to do his thing, and returned to enjoying the moment. "Have you ever lived here?"

"For a while."

"What was it like? I can't decide if it would be amazing or awful."

"A little of both, I guess. I'll tell you all about it on the way back upstate." He shut down the controls. "For now, Zac has a car waiting for us in the parking garage across the street. It'll take about fifteen minutes to get to Henry Porter's office."

She glanced at her watch. It was barely eight in the morning, and she wondered if Maddy had arrived to help Emmie yet. Waiting for Chase to finish whatever he was doing, she unhooked her harness and grabbed her bag. She'd treated herself to the oversized canvas tote at an autumn festival two years ago and was thrilled Naomi had been able to recover it from her wrecked SUV before having it towed to the body shop.

"All right." Chase freed himself from his harness. "Let's go."

She hopped out of the chopper, an abrupt wind gust catching her off guard and sending her hair into a tizzy. She laughed as she tamed it and jogged with Chase toward a door on the roof, then, as they pounded down flight after flight of stairs, she wondered if Chase shared her aversion to elevators. Not that she wouldn't use one, but it wasn't her favorite thing. The idea of potentially being trapped brought a wave of anxiety that she quickly dismissed. The last thing she needed was a panic attack. Walking down the stairs wasn't bad, but by the eighth flight she was seriously considering an elevator for the trip back up, claustrophobia or not.

When they finally emerged from the building, she was instantly struck by the number of people on the street. All of them seemed to be in a hurry, hustling down the sidewalks, vibrating with energy when they reached the corner and had to wait for the light, then surging across the street en masse. Even those who walked with companions moved at a brisk clip, speaking just as rapidly as they walked. Just the thought of living like this every minute of every day exhausted her.

Chase hooked her arm as the light changed and the mob rushed across the street. Horns blared, a man stood on one corner, shouting about something and handing out brochures. When Diana started to reach for one, Chase grabbed her hand and kept it in his. The scent of greasy food from a corner cart combined with the odor of exhaust turned her stomach.

Before she could even soak in all that was going on in the street, Chase was moving into the parking garage and heading for yet another set of stairs. Three flights later, he fished a key from a metal box in the tire well and unlocked a dark-colored sedan.

She pointed toward the tire and quirked an eyebrow at him. "Is that safe?"

"What?" He paused and looked at her across the car's roof. "Keeping the key in the tire well?"

"Yeah, it seems so…"

"Cliché?" He laughed and got in. "It's fine. Zac's guy only dropped it off about ten minutes ago."

As he adjusted the rearview mirror, his smile faded. By the time he buckled his seatbelt and started the car, any sign of good humor had fled. "Hold on."

He gunned the car around three levels, rocketed out of the lot, then slammed to a stop when they hit a traffic jam. His hand hovered over his holstered weapon.

At the squeal of braked behind them, Diana checked the sideview mirror.

A black SUV with two occupants was practically glued to their bumper. "Chase?"

"Yeah."

She braced a hand against the dashboard and resisted the urge to turn and look behind them. "What are we going to do?"

He swiped a hand over his face then floored it the instant the cars started to move. "Since they didn't start shooting, I can only assume they aren't willing to risk a shootout smack in the middle of New York City. If this is their home turf, they may not want to draw attention. So, we'll do the only thing we can do—lose them."

If the congested street was any indication, it seemed that would be easier said than done. "How do you think they found us?"

"I have no idea. But the fact that they did says an awful lot about the assets these people command." When the light turned red a block later, and the cab in front of him stopped short, he slammed on the brakes and muttered to himself.

They inched through block after block. Traffic seemed to move in unison with the crowds of people. Whenever a light turned green, they were off. Whether or not the pedestrians had finished crossing didn't seem to matter. Traffic stopped again. How were they supposed to shake their tail under these circumstances?

"Hang on." When the light changed to green again, Chase stayed where he was. Horns blared behind him. A cab driver two cars back shook his fist and yelled out the window. Still Chase sat, his gaze fixed on the rearview mirror, never shifting. The instant the light turned red, he gunned it, barely nipping through the intersection without getting T-boned by a bus.

Midway through the block, Chase hit the brakes and fishtailed into a parking garage. He rocketed up the ramp so fast she was afraid they might take flight. They skidded around two levels, Diana holding on for dear life, before returning to the bottom floor. He punched it into an open spot just as a compact car pulled out, then rocked to a sudden stop. "Get out. Go!"

She did as instructed, easing the door shut behind her so

as not to draw attention. The screech of brakes, followed by the squeal of tires sounded somewhere above them.

Chase grabbed her hand and took off running.

"Wait. Don't you have to pay."

He paused long enough to lift a brow, grin, and shake his head. "Zac's got a permit."

They didn't try to speak as they weaved their way among pedestrians. When she was too winded to run any farther, she stopped and bent at the waist to catch her breath.

Chase guided her into a gated doorway, then stood guard while they both took a moment to regulate their breathing. "Can you walk another block?"

"Yeah. I'm okay." The burning in her lungs suggested otherwise. As did her aching leg muscles. "I just needed a minute."

"All right. It seems like we lost them, but stay vigilant. Let's just do what we came for and get out of here."

She couldn't agree more.

He clasped her hand, stuck his other hand in his pocket, and did a quick surveillance before starting along the sidewalk.

As they strolled hand in hand, Diana could almost forget they were on the run, but not quite. She watched the other pedestrians and couldn't help but wonder if any of them shouldered the same kind of secrets. "Is it always so…much?"

Chase laughed and looked around absently. "You get used to it after a while and barely even notice. I forget what it's like for someone arriving for the first time."

"It feels so… I don't know…" She struggled for the right word to express the sense of orderly chaos, the frenzy of people and cars and buses. "Alive, I guess."

"That's a good word for it." He looked around then gestured for her to cross the street. "I've traveled a lot, first for the FBI and then with Jameson Investigations, but I've never been anywhere else with the same sense of energy."

"It's incredible." She paused and waited for the light to change, trying to take in everything at once, then surged through the intersection with everyone else, invisible amid the crowd. "But I don't think I'd like to live here."

"It never bothered me. And it's convenient. You can find pretty much anything you need anytime of the day or night."

"I'll take my cabin in the mountains any day. It's peaceful, quiet…"

He shot her a smirk.

"Okay, fine. It is when no one is blowing up cabins, causing rockslides and shooting automatic weapons at you."

"I don't know." He winked, this playful side of him something she was coming to enjoy. "Sounds to me like the city might be safer."

She couldn't help but laugh. If he'd made that claim two days ago, she'd have thought him crazy. Now, well, not so much. "Except for those two guys chasing us."

"Hey, at least they didn't open fire."

She couldn't argue that.

He stopped and looked up at a towering building. "This is it."

Diana followed his gaze. For just an instant, it seemed the building was falling over, and she jerked back.

"Don't worry. That happens occasionally when you look up at them."

A sense of wonder nearly overwhelmed her. "How high up do we have to go?"

He pulled a Post-it note out of his pocket and unfolded it. "Twenty-fifth floor."

"Twe—" Giving up, she just lowered her head and trudged beside him. No sense complaining, though she did briefly consider staying right where she was and letting Chase go up by himself. Twenty-five floors on an elevator did not appeal, but neither did twenty-five flights of stairs, especially after hiking up half a mountain while being shot at.

As if understanding her trepidation, Chase took her hand in his. "Come on. Let's get this over with."

After a quick check at the registration desk, where he discreetly flashed his Jameson Investigation ID and signed in, he crossed the lobby and headed straight for the elevators. She wasn't sure whether to be relieved or horrified. They ascended smoothly at first, then it began to feel like the building was swaying, the elevator with it. She clutched the railing.

"It's okay. It always feels like that."

"Okay, I've decided. I definitely do not want to live in a high-rise." When they finally reached the twenty-fifth floor, and the doors slid open, she stepped out on shaky legs. "My legs feel like rubber."

Chase started to laugh, then his expression went stone-cold. He stepped in front of Diana and pulled his weapon in one fluid motion before she could even register anything amiss. "Stay back."

Placing her back against the wall, she spotted the partially opened door that had caught his attention.

Chase inched forward, weapon held steady in front of him.

Diana kept pace, sliding against the wall slightly behind him to allow him room to maneuver if they were attacked.

When he reached the door with *Henry Porter, Private Investigator* stenciled in bold print, he put a finger to his lips.

As if she'd say anything that might possibly alert any intruders. She rolled her eyes.

He grinned at that—smart aleck—then eased around the doorjamb, weapon first, and toed the door the rest of the way open.

Diana crept into an alcove across from the office, with a clear view of the inside. Either Henry Porter kept his office like a pigsty, or it had been ransacked. If she had to guess, she'd say the latter. Folders and their spilled contents littered the floor, the desk and chair had been overturned, file cabinets hung open with papers scattered everywhere. It seemed whoever had ransacked the office had done so in a fit of rage rather than as part of a methodical search for any kind of information. A robbery? Maybe. But whatever it was almost had to be connected to their investigation. Didn't it?

She watched Chase systematically clear the room, without so much as a glance at the scattered papers. Once he cleared the main office, he entered another room that from her vantage point seemed to be a storage room. It was now filled with a knee-high pile of papers. Banker's boxes had been pulled off shelves and upended or crushed. Metal shelving units had been overturned. She had to wonder if whoever had trashed the place had done so because they couldn't find what they were looking for. Or maybe they'd found what they sought and wrecked the office to cover their tracks and keep anyone from realizing precisely what they'd taken. Either way, there was no chance she and Chase could search through all those papers by themselves and figure out if anything was missing. It would take days. Or longer.

Chase checked the bathroom, then emerged and traded his weapon for his cell phone. He pressed it against his ear and waited in the office doorway, surveying the mess. "Yeah, Zac, the place is trashed."

Diana could only make out the sound of a muffled voice on the other end, no actual words.

"Let us do a cursory search before you call law enforcement, see if we can find anything pertaining to our investigation, but I have to say…" He glanced over his shoulder at the mess. "I'm not optimistic."

Diana had to agree.

"What kind of problem?" He scowled, his gaze shooting to Diana's before his expression turned rock-hard, his blue eyes turning to ice.

Oh, no. Emmie! Muttering came from the other end. Despite straining to hear, Diana couldn't make out what was said. She moved closer, held her breath. *Please, let Emmie be safe.*

"What! No!" His gaze shot to hers, his expression hardening even further. "Absolutely not. No way."

He paused, clenched his fist so tight she was afraid he'd crush the phone.

"We'll be back as soon as we go through the office. Stall him. Please. At least until we have the chance to see if Porter had any evidence of what he'd gotten himself into." He gestured Diana into the office and followed on her heels. "Yeah, thanks."

When he started to move, she splayed a hand against his chest. "What's wrong?"

He closed his eyes, his shoulders sagged and he sighed

before meeting her gaze. "One of Naomi's deputies just called. Someone claiming to be Emmie's father showed up at the sheriff's department demanding to speak with the sheriff. He wants custody of Emmie. Immediately."

No! "They can't give her over to him."

He raked a hand through his hair and turned to the mess in the room. "If we don't find something on him in here, and he can provide a birth certificate or some other proof his claim is legit, they won't have a choice. As it is, they're going to stall him. The deputy told him he's having a hard time reaching Naomi, but that will only buy us so much time. At the end of the day, if Naomi can't talk him into allowing her and Zac to continue providing protective custody for that child, and we can't find any evidence that he's done anything wrong, they're going to have to turn her over."

"Then we'd better find something, because that is not happening. I'll take her on the run myself before allowing that man to get his hands on her without us knowing if he poses a danger."

"All right. Just take a breath. While we sort through this stuff as quickly as possible, Zac has agents scouring the world for anything they can use to keep the guy from taking custody. So far, though, they haven't found anything. He's never been arrested, never mind convicted, of a crime. There are no warrants out for his arrest, no allegations or reports of any kind of domestic abuse, other than what her mother implied when she talked to Naomi."

"Then we'd better get started." She waded into the main room.

"Skip the stuff scattered all over. Presumably, whoever ransacked the place would have gone through that and deemed it unimportant. The police, hopefully in coordination with Zac, can process all of that later."

She stood in the middle of the room and looked around. "Then what are we looking for?"

"A hidey-hole. Someplace he might have stashed stuff they didn't find."

"All right." She struggled to focus on the task at hand when every instinct was begging her to return to Emmie.

"Oh, and for the record." He paused to make eye contact. "If Emmie has to disappear, you won't be going on the run with her yourself. We're in this together."

"Even if it means kidnapping a child?"

"Together. No matter what."

An hour into the search, Chase slammed a file folder on the top of one of the few file cabinets that remained upright. "This is a waste of time."

Diana felt along the bottom of the overturned desk. "Not that I don't agree, but if we give up now and go back with nothing, we're going to have a difficult choice to make."

She didn't need to remind him. He'd already checked in with Zac twice, and Emmie's father had proven his claim. Zac and Naomi were stalling as best they could in a desperate attempt to give Chase and Diana time to find evidence linking Matt Jordan to any crime that they could use to detain him or keep his daughter away from him. So far, they'd found nothing. "There has to be a cubby or safe around here somewhere."

Diana stopped searching, turned a chair upright and flopped onto it. With her hands encased in rubber gloves, so as not to leave any evidence of their search, she used her wrist to push her hair out of her face. She surveyed the room, then frowned and stood. "The few pictures on the walls have all been pulled off, and there's nothing behind them. So where else would you conceal a safe?"

Chase paused, used his shoulder to swipe the sweat from his cheek and looked around. Where could a safe be hidden that whoever had searched would have missed? Every wall was bare, so they... Wait. He surveyed the room. "The floor."

"Huh?"

"You can conceal a safe in the floor, and if whoever wrecked this place came in here in a fit of rage and started tossing things, they may have unwittingly buried it." He stood, grabbed a push broom from the small closet in the bathroom and started sweeping the mess aside. "As I shove this stuff out of the way, you come along behind me and search for anything out of the ordinary."

She jumped up, her energy level seemingly renewed, and kneeled on the floor. She ran her gloved hands along every seam in the builder-grade tile. "What am I looking for?"

"Anything. A raised spot, a place where the tiles don't seem to line up properly, a recessed handle or combination." He bent to turn a coatrack upright. "An area rug you could conceal a door beneath."

She sat back on her feet and surveyed the room, waiting for him to move aside another section of the mess. She tilted her head, narrowed her gaze, then slowly climbed to her feet. "The bathroom."

"What?" He paused and looked over his shoulder.

"Here." She took the broom from him and dragged him to where she'd been kneeling. "Kneel down and look into the bathroom."

He did as she instructed, then leaned down even lower.

While the rest of the rooms were tiled in a high-traffic, durable, but builder-quality commercial tile, the bathroom had laminate flooring. It was probably waterproof, but still, why change it from tile? It could be an optical illusion, but from where he was kneeling, the floor looked off, crooked, the seams running at odd angles, as if whoever had installed it didn't know what they were doing. He stood and cleared the way to the bathroom with Diana at his side.

He searched for an edge of the flooring he could lift, but the trim held the floor panels neatly in place. "Find something I can use to pry this trim off."

Diana took off running.

When his cell phone rang, his first instinct was to ignore it, then he reconsidered. If something was going on with Emmie, they needed to know. At the same time, he did not want to walk out of there without ripping this flooring up. "Hey, Zac, what's up?"

"We're going to have to give her up, Chase."

"Don't do it, Zac. Not yet."

"I'm not going to have a choice. He managed to get before a judge, petition the court for custody."

"What are you talking about? How could he have done that so quickly?"

"Exactly—that's the question we've been asking, too."

The line hummed for a minute while Chase ran through the possibilities. "How does this guy have the kind of resources necessary to get his sorry self in front of a judge on a moment's notice? Who is he?"

"We don't know." The defeat in Zac's voice was something Chase had never heard before. And it scared him. Zac always had a plan B, along with a whole alphabet of additional plans if that one tanked. "He has almost no online presence at all."

"Smart, if you think about it, especially if you're involved in something shady."

Zac blew out a breath. "I'm sorry to say it, Chase, but it looks like he's more than just involved. The kind of power this guy seems to wield doesn't make sense in any kind of legal way."

"Mafia, you think?"

"Not according to any of my sources."

Diana returned and held out a letter opener.

"All right. I'll be back as soon as I check one more spot. Just hold them off as long as you can." He took the letter opener from her and started prying off trim, yanking it free with no concern about the damage he was causing. If they didn't get back there soon and get Emmie, Zac would have to give her up. While he might get away with doing things outside the box sometimes, he was still bound by the law. If he openly flouted the law, he'd lose the backing of the numerous agencies that supported him. Chase understood he couldn't risk that. But Chase could. He could cut ties with Jameson Investigations and let Zac claim he'd gone rogue. But he had to go it alone. No way did he want to involve Diana, since getting caught would most likely result in serious charges, maybe even prison time. Of course, that meant he'd have to take care of Emmie on his own.

A chill raced through him at the thought, but he shook it off. He'd just have to deal with it. He tossed a piece of trim through the doorway into the office, then lifted a piece of flooring, revealing the same commercial tile as the office. "It's not glued down. Just start pulling it up."

The speed at which she moved told him she understood

his sense of urgency, had probably overheard enough of his conversation to get the gist of what was going on.

"Wait. There." She pointed to the section of floor right beneath the piece of laminate he'd just tipped up, then dropped to her knees. "There's a padlock on it."

He tossed the laminate out of the way and kneeled beside her to inspect the lock. A wood hatch was held in place by a recessed clasp with a cheap store-bought padlock. He pulled out his gun. "Go into the office and grab some kind of bag. As soon as this gun goes off, someone will call the police, and we need to be gone before they show up, or we'll be stuck here for hours."

She paused. "What if we don't find anything in there?"

He shrugged off her concern. "We're out of time, anyway. If there's nothing useful in here, we'll have to cut our losses. Zac can't hold Matt Jordan off any longer. If I don't get back there and get Emmie, he's going to have to hand her over."

What—if anything—was concealed beneath that board was going with them. They could figure the rest out later.

The instant she cleared the doorway, he fired. It took three shots to damage the clasp and surrounding wood enough to get it open. He ripped off the lock, tossed it aside and whipped open the trapdoor. A stack of folders, a locked box and a handgun sat in a shallow hole. He jammed the gun in his pocket, mostly because he wouldn't leave it unsecured when they fled, then he stuffed everything else into the thick, black garbage bag Diana held open. "Go. Don't run. Walk at a casual but brisk pace, just like everyone else you saw on the street. Look straight ahead and keep your gaze lowered."

"Won't that look suspicious?"

"Not in New York. Everyone here is in a hurry." He tied the bag as he hurried toward the door. When they emerged from the office, he pulled the door shut behind him. Hopefully, it would buy them time to get away before anyone noticed the ransacked office.

Gawkers had already begun to gather in the hallway, an anxious hum buzzing through the crowd as they tried to determine where the shots had come from. Several people held cell phones to their ears, no doubt calling the police.

Ignoring them, he kept watch on Diana as she hit the button to summon the elevator. Sweat slid down the sides of her face into her hairline, but she maintained her composure. Once they were inside and the doors had closed, she slumped against the wall. "Do you think they'll try to stop us on our way out?"

"Hopefully not, but just in case…here." He thrust the bag into her hands so he could get to his weapon if needed, then handed her the key to the car. "Hang on to that bag no matter what happens. And if I get stopped, you keep going. Once you're a safe distance away, call Zac and tell him what happened. He'll send someone to pick you up."

"But—"

"No *buts.*" The light above the door counted down the floors—four left. "Whatever's in that bag might save Emmie's life. You hold on to it and get out of here no matter what. Do you understand me?"

She bristled, and he braced himself for the argument they had no time for. Then she looked up at the numbers flying by too quickly and yet not quickly enough and clutched the bag close. Maybe she'd learned to trust him a little over the past few days, or maybe she agreed with leaving him behind if needed. Either way, it didn't matter as long as she went. Of course, there was always the possibility she'd ignore him and do what she wanted when the time came.

But he had no more time to contemplate it as the doors slid open to the lobby. People behind the desk were busy fielding phone calls, no doubt from concerned residents wanting to know where the gunshots had come from. A small group of security guards huddled beside the desk as their supervisor issued orders. A police cruiser pulled up out front, lights flashing, and angled toward the curb, blocking the sedan they'd arrived in. "Turn left out of their path and start walking."

Diana hit the door, pale and shaking, and hung a left without glancing toward the officers rushing into the building. She kept the bag clutched against her. Even to a trained observer, he believed she appeared frightened but not threatening, just a nervous bystander hurrying to get out of harm's way.

He followed her to the end of the block, keeping his hands free, then surged across the street with the first light that changed. Once they crossed, he hooked her arm with his and pulled her close. "You okay?"

"Fine. You?"

"Good." He chanced a quick look behind him, but no one seemed to be in pursuit. He stopped at the next corner and hailed a cab, then gave the driver the address of the building with the helipad.

Diana looked out the back window as more police officers arrived on the scene a block behind them. "What about the car?"

"Zac'll send someone for it later."

She gestured toward the bag. "Did you get to see what anything was?"

"Nah. I was in too much of a hurry. We'll check it out once we're in the air." They made it back to the chopper without incident, but he didn't dare breathe a sigh of relief until they were in the air and leaving New York City behind.

"What's going to happen when they figure out where the shots came from?"

He shrugged. "It depends on what we find in the bag. Zac will most likely hold off on calling the police about the vandalism in Porter's office until after we know what we have here, if we have anything. If no one else reports it, we should have time to go through everything and figure out what we're dealing with before anyone else discovers the damage."

"What about the police crawling all over that building right now?"

"Most of the people in the hallway seemed confused, as if they weren't quite sure which direction the shots came from. Three shots, in rapid succession. Some of them might even try to say it was something else." The responding officers would have to search the building, though, make sure no one had been killed or injured. They would come across the damaged lock and clasp along with the gaping hole in the floor soon enough. "Let's just hope we can find something before Zac has to explain what happened."

He keyed the radio to let Zac know they were on their way.

Diana studied the horizon while Chase flew toward the mountains, the autumn colors dappling the landscape no longer of interest.

A flash of light blinded him for a moment, and then another chopper appeared out of nowhere and opened fire.

EIGHT

"Hold on to the bag." Chase banked hard to the left.

Diana maintained a death grip on the garbage bag, then lost it when he yanked them back the other way.

"Zac," Chase yelled into the radio. "We're under fire. I'm hit. I'm going to have to put her down."

Down? Wait. What? He did mean he was going to land the helicopter, right? Not crash? Diana started to hyperventilate. If they had to run once they *landed*, she would struggle to do so, being hindered by the garbage bag. It was awkward and unwieldy, not to mention not very sturdy. If it ripped, they'd lose whatever they'd just risked their lives for, along with any chance of helping Emmie. No way was she losing this information.

As Chase yelled coordinates to Zac, she pried her hand from the rail she'd been clutching and searched for some way to secure the documents. Her canvas tote bag was in the footwell. She upended it, dumping the contents onto the floor. As everything rolled and bounced, she grabbed her wallet—at least they'd be able to identify her if she didn't make it—then stuffed it into the tote, along with the garbage bag full of documents and the lockbox. It was a tight fit, but she managed to cram everything in and get the zipper closed, then slung the bag over her head and one arm, unbuckled her seat belt for one second, then resecured it over the bag. If they had to run, at least she'd be ready.

"Get down!" Chase managed to shove Diana's head down while wrestling the chopper's controls, as the stick he held vibrated violently against his efforts.

A barrage of bullets tore through the fuselage.

Diana cowered lower, wrapped her arms over her head and prayed for a way out of this.

Chase fought for control.

She concentrated on taking deep, steady breaths. They were going down. She'd already accepted that. Her only hope for control would come after they landed. Landed, not crashed. The bag they'd absconded with had to be protected at all costs, and they had to survive if they were going to save Emmie. As it was, this had probably slowed them down enough that Emmie would be turned over to her father.

She rubbed at the ache in her heart.

"You okay?"

"What?" she yelled over a cacophony of screaming alarms.

"Are you hurt?" She turned her head, still keeping it low, and realized Chase was watching her. "Oh, yeah. No. I'm not hurt, just scared for Emmie."

He nodded, seeming to understand. "Hold on."

Smoke poured from somewhere, obscuring her view out his side window—probably for the best, considering how fast the ground must be rushing up at them. She choked down the fear. It wouldn't help them, and she needed her head on straight when they hit the ground. If they survived the crash, there would still be the gunmen to deal with.

"I'm putting it down where they can't land too close, but it's gonna be rough."

He might buy them a few minutes, but they'd have to be ready to run right away.

"Get ready, Diana. This is going to hurt." Vibrations tore through the chopper. Alarms blared. Zac yelled something to them from the radio, but she couldn't make out what. Hopefully, it wasn't important.

She squeezed her eyes closed. "God, please get us through this. Please, guide Chase's hand and help us land gently and escape so we can save that little girl."

"Amen," Chase added quietly as he lost his battle for control.

The chopper hit the ground hard and rolled, tumbling through trees and brush, tearing it apart. The odor of gas hit her just as flames erupted, engulfing everything behind them. She fought the overpowering instinct to stiffen, forced her legs to remain limp. She'd seen too many accident victims with broken legs and shattered feet from bracing them against the floor.

And then, for just a fraction of a second, everything went completely still—no sounds, no odors, nothing but silence. A sense of peace came over her. She closed her eyes, relaxed her body...and then chaos erupted.

Two things registered amid the bedlam. One, the chopper had finally stopped rolling, and two, she was alive. "Oh, God, thank You," she whispered. She held on tightly to whatever she could reach, inhaled a deep breath of the acrid smoke and coughed while she waited for the world to stop spinning.

As soon as the sensation eased, she whipped off her harness, sat up tentatively and took stock. She was banged up with a new set of aches and pains, but she could move, which they'd better do before the other chopper found somewhere to land and their attackers resumed their pursuit.

A sudden sense of rocking assailed her. Vertigo? She froze, kept perfectly still, listened and felt the sway of the chopper.

No, they were definitely moving. She inched up until she could see out through a crack in the fuselage, and her breath caught in her throat. "I think we're in a lake."

Silence.

"Chase?"

Nothing.

Her heart stuttered to a stop, then ratcheted into overdrive. "Chase?"

She turned, wiggled out of her seat and pulled aside a large flat piece of metal, slicing her palm. That was the least of her problems, though, so she ignored it.

Chase was still buckled into his seat, but the seat had detached, leaving him lying on his side, head cocked at an uncomfortable angle, blood flowing from a gash on his temple.

"Chase!" She started toward him, and her bag snagged on something, yanking the strap taut against her throat, choking her. She stopped, and inched back to loosen the strap. Without thinking, her gaze riveted on Chase, she slipped the strap over her head, disentangled her arm, then froze. The bag was still caught, and she couldn't pull it free. They were in a lake, possibly sinking, portions of the chopper still on fire...

She had to get Chase out, then get to the bag. If she couldn't tug it free, she could always unzip it and pull out the garbage bag. Okay, one step at a time. That was how they would make it through this.

At least now, she was in familiar territory. A wild helicopter chase, sneaking into buildings, searching for evidence, running from gun-wielding assassins—all of that was way out of her comfort zone. Saving someone from burning wreckage—that, she could do. That, she was trained for.

Needing to make sure she could find it again, she twisted behind her and hooked the bag's strap over a metal bar protruding from the side of the chopper, which was now above her. She took a quick couple of seconds to get her bearings and assess the situation. The gaping hole in what had been the top of the chopper and was now the side would be easy enough to escape through as soon as she got Chase free.

She reached him and assessed the head wound. Not too deep, but bleeding profusely. With nothing in sight to use as a bandage, she'd have to leave it for now. She checked his neck—it seemed okay. As much as she hated to move him, she had no choice. "Chase! You have to wake up. I…"

I…what? Need you? Yes, and she hadn't realized how much. A sob wrenched free, surprising her. She hadn't even realized she was crying. Her strong feelings for him had crept up on her, ambushed her at the worst possible moment. "Please, Chase, stay with me."

As gently as possible, she straightened his head, then held it in place between her hand and her cheek and used her free hand to unclip the harness. Thankfully, it opened easily and she was able to untangle him from the straps.

She grabbed the piece of metal she'd moved from atop him and slid it toward her, then turned it over so the sharp edges angled down away from Chase. Smoke stung her eyes, and she squinted as she tilted him to the side, got her arms beneath him and hauled him toward the makeshift backboard. "Chase. Hey, Chase. Come on. Wake up. This would be a lot easier with a little help, you know."

Wheezing, she tried to wedge the metal into a position where it would be braced still, so she could wrestle him onto it. When she managed to get his upper body, head and neck somewhat stabilized, she decided that was good enough. Leaving his legs and one arm hanging off, with the rest of him at a cockeyed angle, she managed to maneuver him through the torn fuselage and into the lake.

She dove through after him and breathed a sigh of relief when her feet hit the bottom. She stood, the water only waist-deep, and guided him toward the shore.

The sound of an approaching chopper had her abandoning all caution. She hauled herself out of the lake, scooped Chase beneath the arms and dragged him up the beach, beneath a massive pine tree, and behind a group of boulders. Then she quickly ran out and used a branch full of dead leaves to erase the footprints and drag marks. The ruse would never work if a trained tracker sought them, but hopefully, it would do well enough to keep anyone from spotting them from the sky until she could get that bag, treat Chase's injuries and get them to safer ground.

She checked his pulse—still strong. Breathing not labored. He'd be okay for a few minutes until she could contact Zac and—

Ice raced through her veins. They couldn't contact Zac. They couldn't contact anyone, because Chase had set his phone aside to charge, and she'd dumped her own out with the contents of her bag. Now, both were lost somewhere amid the wreckage. She'd have to see if she could find one of them, along with something to use for bandages, when she went back in after the bag. At least the flames had changed course. The wreckage and fuel floating atop the water still burned, as did the path they'd torn through the forest, but the part of the chopper they'd been stuck in seemed to be out of the fire's path...at least for the moment.

Diana braced herself to run back into the lake, listened intently for the sound of the chopper overhead. What if it was Zac's men looking for them? They'd easily see the plume of smoke, but so would their pursuers. No way was she exposing herself until she knew who was out there.

"Hey, Marty, over here." A man emerged from a trail in the woods a few feet from where she and Chase were hidden, then stopped short, propped his hands on his hips and stared at the wreckage. Judging from his business suit, he was definitely not a nature lover who just happened to be there when the crash occurred.

She ducked lower, held her breath and prayed that a disoriented Chase didn't choose that moment to wake and give away their position. She put a hand atop his chest, hoping it would still him if he did.

Marty followed on his partner's heels, stopped beside him and let out a low whistle. "Do you think they died in the crash?"

The guy shrugged. "The boss said make sure."

She quietly unholstered Chase's gun, flipped off the safety and held her breath.

"All righty, Jim. Looks like one of us is going swimming. And it ain't gonna be me." Marty surveyed the damaged chopper in the lake, then the surrounding woods, and winced. "Too much nature gives me the creeps."

"I know what you mean." Jim toed off his shoes and

stuck his socks inside them, then rolled up his pant legs and started to wade toward the chopper.

Marty stuck his hands in his pockets, then turned to look over his shoulder.

Diana ducked lower, careful to keep them in view through the brush. She had to get back into the wreckage for her bag, but she didn't want to have to shoot anyone to do so. Nor did she want to get shot. She'd wait and see if Jim emerged with the files. If not, she'd wait for them to take off before going back in. If so, well, she'd cross that bridge if she came to it.

Jim emerged after what felt like hours, but was probably not more than a couple of minutes. He was empty-handed, and started toward the shore. "Great, now what?"

"Now, we get to hunt them down like a couple of animals and put them out of our misery before they can escape these woods." Marty offered a vicious grin. "The guy's probably not an issue, but Jordan said the woman might have seen him when she was running from the blaze, so she's gotta go."

"Might have?" Jim kept his head on a swivel while he got himself back together.

"It don't matter. Either way, the broad's done for." Marty pointed toward the trail they'd emerged from. "They must have gone up that trail and turned the other way, where it branched off."

"What about the kid?"

"Jordan's about to get her, says it's practically a done deal."

"Yeah, but I still don't get why he's going to keep her." With one last glance around the clearing, Jim started back toward the trail. "How can he be so sure she ain't already ratted him out?"

Marty fell into step beside him. "The kid barely talks as it is, but when he couldn't find her in the cabin, he called out that he'd kill her if she said anything. Since she'd just witnessed him kill her mother and that PI she hired, I'm pretty sure she believed him. If she's got half a brain, she'll keep her trap shut and do what she's told. Why kill her if he don't have to? The kid's worth millions. Better to stash her in the storage unit until the pickup, then we can all wash our hands of the whole thing and move on to spending our fortune."

"You got that right." They laughed, long and loud, as they trudged up the trail into the forest.

Suddenly, the idea of shooting them wasn't quite as abhorrent. Not in the head or chest or anything vital, but maybe a kneecap. She begged forgiveness for the thought. They would get out of this with no one else getting hurt or killed. Somehow. God willing.

Chase startled and jerked upright, then squeezed his eyes closed and waited for the world to stop spinning. He clenched a fist...and froze. Was that dirt beneath him? And were those trees he'd seen spinning around him? He slitted his eyes open and peeked out. Thankfully, everything stayed put, but he was still sitting on the ground surrounded by trees. How had that happened? Hadn't they been in the chopper? Pain tore through his head.

Right. He remembered now. Someone was following them. And, what? He struggled to chase away the lingering confusion. They'd been attacked, shot down, crashed. *Diana!*

He scanned his surroundings—trees, brush, boulders— but where was the chopper? Or whatever remained of it?

He pressed his fingers against the stabbing pain in his temple and pulled them away covered in blood. How had he gotten here? Had he been thrown from the chopper in the crash? He had to get to Diana. But where was she?

He stood slowly, careful to assess his injuries as he moved. Aches, pains, some bruised ribs that hopefully weren't broken, and the pounding headache. While he was still a bit lightheaded and unsteady on his feet, the worst of the vertigo had passed, and he could remain upright.

He stood where he was and listened intently for any sign of Diana...or their attackers. Nothing. A cool breeze rippled through the trees, helping to clear more of the cobwebs. He rounded a grouping of boulders and emerged from the tree line, then stopped dead in his tracks. The chopper was lying on its side in the lake, partially submerged, fuel still burning. His breath caught; his legs threatened to buckle.

Diana!

If he'd been able to suck in a full breath, between the possibly busted ribs and the gut-wrenching fear coursing through him, he'd have called out to her with no thought for who might overhear. What did that say about his current state? It seemed to hint at something personal, something he didn't dare examine if he wanted to function well enough to find her.

He jogged toward the water's edge, fear threatening to consume him. Without bothering to take off his shoes, he plunged into the water just as Diana poked her head out from the wreckage.

She frowned at him. "What are you doing?"

The relief he felt took his knees out from under him. As his entire world crumbled around him, he was stunned to realize just how far he'd fallen without even realizing.

He'd told himself he could never have feelings for anyone else, had convinced himself he'd never get close to anyone again, and yet, somehow, this stubborn, argumentative, incredibly courageous woman had finagled her way past his barriers and straight into his heart. Could he ever love her? He had no idea. But for the first time in eight long, torturous years, something in him opened to the possibility. "I couldn't find you."

"So, what? You're my knight in shining armor staggering to my rescue?" She waggled her eyebrows, but her deep scowl belied her attempt to lighten the mood.

"Something like that, I guess." He forced a laugh as he reached her and held his arms out to help her into the water. "Want to tell me what's wrong? Other than the obvious, of course."

"Thanks. And yes, but let's get out of the open first." She gripped his hand, balanced herself against the fuselage, then turned and yanked her bag out from the debris. She reached in again for a first-aid kit and shoved it into his hands.

"You got the files?"

"Yeah." She patted the bag. "I've got them."

"You're..." Incredible? Unbelievable? Amazing? "Something else."

"Ha!" She waded beside him, scanning the beach as she surged through the water with the bag held high enough to keep it from getting wet. "I'm not sure if I should be flattered or offended."

Neither was he, so he kept his thoughts to himself. It felt like she already had him turned upside down. If he wasn't careful, she might be his undoing. "Any sign of our attackers?"

"Yeah." Her eyes hardened, and her expression sobered. "Two men, Marty and Jim...?"

She let the question hang, but he shook his head. He'd never heard the names before, and without last names, there would be no quick way to identify them. "Where'd they go?"

She pointed toward a trail that led into the forest. "They said Jordan is about to get Emmie. We have to get to her, have to stop him. But I don't know how we're going to get out of here or how we're going to find her if we do. Maybe we should split up. They might be willing to leave you behind, but they have orders not to leave this forest without killing me."

"Why? And for the record, we are not separating, so forget about that." He stepped onto dry land, his legs suddenly weighing a thousand pounds as he struggled back toward the tree line, where they would have at least some semblance of cover.

"Jordan thinks I saw him running from the cabin the night I found Emmie. He wants me shut up so I can't testify against him." She led him straight to the spot he'd awoken in.

His mind faltered as he realized that there was no way he could have been thrown from the chopper and just happened to land here, under the tree and behind the boulders. However he'd gotten there, he'd had help. "How'd you know to come to this spot?"

She swiped her hair, tangled and matted, away from her face and unzipped the bag. "It's where I left you after I pulled you from the chopper."

He looked back in the direction they'd come, as if the brush, trees and boulders were invisible and he could see clear to the mangled remains of the chopper in the lake. "How'd you get me out of that mess and all the way up here?"

"It wasn't easy." She patted his rock-hard abs, sending a jolt of agony through his battered ribs. "You might want to lose a few pounds, buddy, if you expect me to be hauling you around the wilderness."

He grinned through the pain. "I'll keep that in mind."

"You do that." She pulled the garbage bag from her bag, checked it for damage, then stood, contemplating it.

"We can't go through it right now." No matter how badly he wanted to. "We have to move before Jordan's goons come back."

She sat on the ground, folded her legs and began tucking the garbage bag back away. "I agree we can't unpack everything right now. We can't take the chance of having to leave it behind if those men show back up. But we are not going anywhere. Not yet, anyway. You relayed our last coordinates to Zac. He will already have agents on their way. So…" She patted the ground next to her. "Now, we sit and wait, because if his agents have to hunt us through this forest, it's going to take us even longer to get back to Emmie."

His mouth fell open, opened and closed like a landed trout a few times, then he snapped it shut without saying anything. Apparently, a near brush with death hadn't softened her stance on arguing with him.

She didn't bother to look up at him as she started to pull the zipper closed. It snagged on something, and she caught her bottom lip between her teeth while she worked it back and forth trying to free it. "Are you just going to stand there fuming all day?"

He continued to stare at her, that long, tangled auburn

hair framing her delicate features no matter how many times she shoved it away, a gesture that had probably become automatic, she did it so often.

"Look, Chase." Giving up on the zipper for a moment, she looked up, and her gaze slammed straight through him. "I've given in a good number of times and done things your way, even when I wasn't completely sure it was the right thing to do. I accepted you might know better than me, and that wasn't easy for me. Now, please, stop being so thick-headed for once, and listen to me. You're bleeding fairly profusely from your head and you're soaking wet. And that's not even mentioning what other injuries you might have. You are also swaying on your feet, right now—and for the record, if you tip over, I'm moving out of the way and letting you fall. We need to get your head patched up and sit still for one hot minute. Then, after we've tended to your wounds, dried off in the sun for a little while and taken a second to catch our breath, we can reevaluate the situation. I figure those guys already searched here. They'll probably bumble around in the woods for at least a little while before coming back this way. Hopefully, by then, your boss will have shown up with the cavalry."

"And you're really okay with sitting here and waiting? I thought you'd be desperate to get back to Emmie."

A dark look crossed her face. "I am. And trust me, if getting to her was possible right now, I'd already be moving. But those men said that Jordan is on the verge of getting her. Hopefully, Zac will be able to stop that, but if he can't…

"They seemed to think he had good reason to keep her alive for now, but she's definitely still in danger—especially if he thinks she told us anything." Her lips tightened and she took a slow breath. "But I can't focus on that

right now. Not when there's nothing I can do. The best way
to keep her safe is to make sure the two of us get out of here
alive with whatever we found in that office."

Without another word, he sat down next to her, stretched
out his legs and leaned back on his hands. He tilted his
face to the sun and contemplated his options. The more he
thought about it, the righter she seemed.

Frustrated with the stuck zipper, she slammed the bag
aside. He sat up straighter, put the bag on his legs and
smoothed the fabric on either side of the zipper, then wiggled the zipper back and forth. "So, did you?"

She blew out a breath. "Did I what?"

He glanced at her, willing her to see the truce in his eyes.
"Did you see Jordan running from the cabin that night?"

She shook her head, though he couldn't tell if it was in
answer or simply frustration. "I didn't see anyone."

The zipper came free, and he slid it and held the bag
back out to her.

She took it and set it aside. "Thanks."

"You bet."

Then she turned to face him. "Why don't you let me treat
that wound before you end up passing out on me?"

He folded his legs then turned and leaned his back
against a tree trunk. "Fine."

She rummaged through the first-aid kit, took out bandages and saline, then set aside the kit and scooted closer
until she was kneeling in front of him. "I'm going to clean
this first, then I'll bandage it up. It doesn't appear to be too
deep, but it'll need stitches. If no one shows up to rescue us
or kill us in the next few minutes, I can put in the stitches
myself, if you want. It might leave a worse scar than if you

had it done at the hospital, though. Wouldn't want to mess up that pretty mug of yours."

She smiled at him, her fingers ice-cold as she ran them along his temple to smooth his hair out of the way. Her hand lingered, her touch soft, delicate.

He searched her eyes for some hint she might be feeling any of the connection between them that he'd begun to feel. There was kindness in her eyes, and firm resolve. Beyond that…he just wasn't sure. "Thank you."

"For what?" She glanced away, soaked a bandage in saline and went to work cleaning his cut.

He gripped her chin and brought her gaze back to meet his. "For saving my life."

"No problem. We're in this together, right?" Her breathless response finally brought a bit of comfort he might not be alone in his attraction.

"Right. Partners."

This time, when she went to work quietly stitching his head, the silence between them became comfortable rather than strained. But he couldn't stop himself from breaking it. "Those guys…you heard them say that Zac and Naomi would have to give Emmie over to her father?"

He didn't really want to think about it at all, couldn't bear the thought of her being with that monster, but it was a situation they'd have to face. Then he saw Diana's face crumble. He reached out and caught a tear just as it tipped over one darkened eyelash. "I'm sorry—I shouldn't have brought it up. Why don't we concentrate on getting out of here instead of worrying ourselves with what-ifs?"

She nodded, sniffed and swiped the tears from her eyes with the back of her wrist. "I'm trying, but I can't help it.

My thoughts keep wandering down that same dark alley, no matter how hard I try to pull them out."

"I understand how that feels, believe me."

She stiffened. "I'm so sorry. I didn't think... I should have realized."

"Hey." He reached for her free hand. "It's okay."

"I can't imagine what you must be going through right now."

"I'm sure you're just as upset as I am. Unfortunately, you were right when you said that there isn't anything we can do about it from here."

"Can I ask you something?" She narrowed her gaze as she concentrated on neat, precise stitches.

"Sure, but I can't promise I'll answer."

"Fair enough." She tied off one stitch and began the next, her gaze carefully averted. "What were you protecting that child from?"

There was no need to specify which child she meant. His first instinct was to clam up and say nothing. But it seemed they'd passed that point somewhere along the line. Still, that part of the story wasn't his to tell. "What has Naomi told you about her past?"

She froze in midstitch and finally met his gaze. "Oh, no. Please, tell me it wasn't her child."

Tears he had no hope of stopping leaked from the corners of his eyes. Hopefully, his sister would forgive him for what he was about to reveal, because he wasn't going to lie to Diana. He was going to share the whole ugly truth. "She was a detective in New York City, and her husband was a prosecutor with the DA's office. There was a case, a big-time drug dealer, they were both part of. The case fell apart when several witnesses disappeared and threats were made against the families of everyone involved—Naomi, her husband, her partner, the judge… Well, you get the idea."

She nodded, already beginning to cry. "I do. Yes."

"So to make a long, ugly story short enough for me to bear telling it, after they took out Naomi's husband, my wife and I were assigned to protect Johnny. We didn't usually work together, but the powers that be made an exception that time because Johnny had just lost his father, and it would make it easier for him to be with people he knew. That, and Naomi begged us."

He squeezed his eyes closed against the memory. "And we failed."

"I am so very sorry, Chase. My heart breaks for everyone involved. I knew Naomi had suffered some tragedy in the past, could see the pain in her eyes at times, but I never asked—maybe because I didn't want to talk about my own past. But I should have. I should have tried to offer comfort."

"She doesn't talk about it. If you'd pressed her, she probably would have pulled away. Maybe your instincts were spot on, and you did exactly what was right for your friendship."

She smiled through the tears at that, then taped a bandage in place over his head wound. "There, that's about the best I can do. It might not be the most inconspicuous scar, but at least you won't look like Frankenstein's monster."

"Thank you. I appreciate that."

"Sure." She checked for signs of a concussion, looked at his bruised ribs, then repacked the first-aid kit, set it aside and started to stand.

He gripped her wrist before she could move. "Please. Just sit here with me for a few minutes."

She studied him for a long moment, then turned and sat beside him.

He wrapped an arm around her and pulled her close, and she rested her head against his shoulder. He could have sat like that for hours, inhaling the scent of nature clinging to her, feeling the tickle of her hair against his cheek, drawing comfort and strength from the weight of her at his side, from the knowledge she now knew his whole ugly truth. Not only hadn't she judged him, but she'd also shown compassion.

He'd learned to appreciate that about her, how she always seemed able to put herself in someone else's shoes. She had more empathy than anyone he'd ever met. She was selfless, brave, sensitive. And the fact that she fit perfectly tucked beneath his arm was an added bonus he should probably not think too hard about.

Sadly, he only got a few minutes reprieve before the sound of a chopper intruded on the moment.

She sighed. "Friend or foe?"

"Hard to tell, but I guess we'll figure it out if they start shooting." Was he going to sit there until they did? Lost in thoughts of something that could never be? No. As much as he'd like to indulge in a moment of peace, they had to be prepared for whatever would come next, be it rescue or attack.

"Get ready." He eased her upright, then stood and reached for his weapon. It was gone. That's what he got for losing his senses over not being able to find Diana when he woke. He hadn't even noticed his gun was missing until this moment.

"I'm sorry. I had to borrow it. Those men were here, and you were unconscious and unable to defend yourself, and I didn't want them to get the bag, and well…" Her pale cheeks reddened as she held the weapon out to him.

And with that vision of her standing over him as protector, he realized how much he'd come to trust her in their situation, had come to rely on her input, and he plunged right over the precipice where he'd been so precariously balanced.

NINE

Maintaining her composure when she'd first spotted Chase entering the lake hadn't been easy. Diana had been so thrilled to see him up and walking, she'd nearly thrown herself out of the burning wreckage into his arms. Thankfully, she'd regained control of her senses before making a fool of herself. Still, she'd never been so relieved as when the Jameson Investigations chopper landed in a nearby clearing and several pretty scary-looking agents—who Chase, thankfully, instantly recognized—emerged from the woods to rescue them. She still wasn't sure if that relief had come from being found or from the opportunity to distract herself from her growing feelings for Chase Mitchell.

Her gaze skipped to him pacing the safe house dining room that had been set up as a conference room. The long table was surrounded by seats mostly filled with agents sorting through various papers and information on laptops as they all awaited Zac's arrival, some more patiently than others.

"Pacing isn't going to get him here any faster, you know," Angela said without looking up from her screen. She started to type, faster than anyone Diana had ever seen, then sighed and, without missing a key stroke, used her foot to shove out the chair between her and Diana. "Sit. Now. You're distracting me."

He shot her a dirty look but dropped onto the chair, picked up a pen and started tapping it against the table. "We should have heard from him by now. The hearing should have ended over an hour ago."

Angela finally stopped typing and put a hand over his to still the tapping. "He's on his way."

Diana studied him—it was easier to think about him than it was to let her mind wander to Emmie. What did that say about her current state of mind?

Chase folded his arms on the table and lay his head down on them.

Diana reached for him, intent on soothing him, then thought better of the idea and let her hand drop into her lap.

Naomi shot her a knowing smile from across the table.

Heat flared in Diana's cheeks, and she barely resisted the urge to yell out "it's not what you think." Because, it was exactly what Naomi probably thought. Somewhere over the past few days, Diana's view of Chase had turned to something more than just a partner, more even than just a friend.

He'd stood between Emmie and danger more than once with no thought for his own well-being, had risked his own safety so Diana and Emmie could escape when they'd gone over the mountainside what seemed like ages ago. When the gunmen had run them off the road, he'd done so again, with no hesitation at all. A warrior. That's what he reminded her of. Filled with honor and valor and courage. Not to mention those rugged good looks that would certainly turn a woman's head. If she was being honest with herself—

She cut off the thought. At the moment, she was better off lying to herself. But was that a sin? To lie to one's self?

God, please help me through this, lead me down the path
You want me to follow, the road that will lead to saving
this little girl. Please.

The front door burst open, then slammed so hard everyone looked up from what they were doing. Zac stormed into the room a moment later and threw his briefcase across the room and onto the floor. His entire face flamed red. He didn't make eye contact with anyone as he dropped onto the seat at the head of the table, propped his elbows, lowered his face into his hands and said softly, "They took her."

Chase exploded from his chair, knocking it to the floor behind him, and pointed a finger at Zac. "How could you let that happen? You were supposed to protect her."

Diana surged to her feet and grabbed his arm—to offer him comfort, borrow his strength, keep him from running out half-cocked? She had no idea.

Mason Payne moved in behind him. "Chase. Sit. Calm down, and let us tell you what happened."

His face turned nearly purple as he whirled on Mason. "I don't care—"

Mason gripped his shoulder, handed him what looked like a cell phone, then leaned close and whispered, "I put a tracker on her."

Chase looked him in the eye, and when Mason nodded, he pocketed the phone and swiped a hand over his beard.

Apparently realizing what he'd said had dampened Chase's rage, at least for the moment, Mason bent and righted Chase's chair, then guided him back into it.

When Diana started to pull away, Chase gripped her hand in his and gestured for her to sit, lacing their fingers together like they were a lifeline to keep him tethered to reality.

Angela, who'd disappeared sometime during Chase's outburst, reappeared and set a tray filled with mugs and two pots of coffee on the table, giving everyone a much-needed reprieve to take a breath and calm down while they passed out coffee.

Once everyone settled, as much as they could with the tension still sizzling through the room, Zac stood, hands splayed on the table, head lowered between his arms. When he did lift his head to face them, his expression was chiseled in stone, but his eyes held such pain, Diana had to turn away.

"Let me start by saying..." His gaze landed on Chase. "Even though I shouldn't have to, that I did everything in my considerable power to keep the judge from awarding Matt Jordan custody of Emmie."

He calmly walked to where he'd thrown his briefcase, picked it up and returned to his spot at the table. His hands shook as he unlocked it and removed a stack of file folders. He kept one and passed the rest to his right. As the folders made their way around the table, he spread his open on the table in front of him. "Our attorneys argued everything imaginable to keep Emmie in our custody, and Jordan's lawyers shot every one of our arguments down."

This time, when his gaze landed on Chase, Chase stiffened.

"Lawyers?" He finally released his grip on Diana's hand to shuffle through the pages in his folder, as Diana did the same.

"An entire team."

"This is Matt Jordan?" Chase pulled out a picture of a short, stocky pit bull of a man. "Who is this guy?"

"That's what we're hoping the information you and

Diana unearthed will tell us." Zac gestured toward the empty seat, where Angela hadn't sat back down after getting coffee. "Angela is copying everything you brought back as we speak. She'll have a file for each of us within the next few minutes. Everyone in this room is to set what you're doing aside to comb through those files, read every single word. We just need one provable offense to have Jordan picked up and get Emmie out of his grasp."

Diana's heart tripped at the thought. "What if you can't find him?"

Zac looked at Mason, then Chase, then back to her. "We'll find him. In the meantime, we brought CPS in, but there was nothing they could do. Emmie was in perfect health, no signs of abuse, no signs of neglect, no reason at all to remove her from Jordan's home and take custody of her. His lawyers argued that being unnaturally quiet and refusing to talk was caused by the trauma of losing her mother and the attacks on her, as well as our failing to keep her out of harm's way rather than any long-term abuse on his part. Dr. Rogers couldn't come up with a single argument to keep her, and believe me, he tried."

"What about the bruises on her arm?" a woman halfway down the table asked.

Zac was already shaking his head. "That was one of the few things Emmie said—the bad man did it on the night of the fire. Then she clammed up. She never specified whether or not Jordan was the bad man."

"Great." Chase flipped a page, reading intently.

Though it hurt more than she could bear to ask, Diana had to know. "How did Emmie react to him? Was she afraid? Did she put up a fuss?"

Zac's sympathetic frown told her all she needed to know.

"She didn't respond to him at all, simply walked away when they sent her with him, head down. She didn't utter one word."

"And no one found that unusual?" she argued.

"Not after all she's been through these past few days. We even tried to hold her in witness protection, pleaded that she was in danger as her mother's killer had already tried on numerous occasions to either abduct or kill her."

Chase glanced up. "And?"

"His lawyers argued that Jordan was wealthy and could hire a private security firm to keep her safe. He didn't need us to provide his daughter with protection, and before anyone says anything…" He held up his hands to ward off all the arguments he'd clearly already thought of. "Maddy Hunter practically begged the judge not to return Emmie to her father, and even she couldn't convince him."

Diana left her folder untouched, wouldn't have been able to focus even if she'd tried. "What about Naomi? Emmie's mother went to her begging for help, told her Jordan was into something illegal and asked for protective custody for her daughter."

"And I testified to exactly that, all of it," Naomi replied. "Nothing. The judge said if Cameron Jordan was that concerned for her daughter's safety, she'd have asked for protective custody the first time she met with me instead of leaving. Plus, she'd hurled accusations about her husband, but they were vague, and she didn't provide me with any concrete evidence to back up her claims." Naomi lifted her hands to her sides. "Trust me, Diana, I fought tooth and nail, but in the end, well, even I wasn't convinced there was any legal merit to removing Emmie from Jordan's home."

"Except she's not going to Jordan's home. She's going to

a storage unit where they will hold her until they get their payday." As soon as the team had come to pick them up in the helicopter, Diana had given them the full rundown of the conversation she'd heard between Marty and Jim in the forest. "Does that do anything to change things? Can you use that to try again?"

Zac shook his head. "You were the only one to overhear the conversation. Chase was unconscious, so he can't even corroborate your story. And even if he could, we don't know who those men are, don't have proof that they actually work for Jordan. They could have been exaggerating or making it up."

Chase slapped the folder closed and scoffed. He shook his head as he met Zac's stare. "The judge was dirty."

Zac shrugged. "Maybe. Or maybe he was threatened or coerced. Either way, he refused to back down."

Chase rocked back on the chair and spread his arms wide. "Okay, so now what?"

"Now, we find some way to get her back."

"Oh, we have a way." Angela strode into the room, tossing folders to each of them as she went. "I skimmed some of this while I was copying it. Open your folders and start reading while I get this up on the screen. Lack of evidence of Jordan's crimes wasn't Henry Porter's problem."

"Then what was?" Zac asked as he opened his folder.

"He had plenty of evidence, but most of it was obtained illegally. He was afraid to go to the DA with it, because Jordan has friends in high places. The case against him would have to be airtight, or he'd be able to swing things his way."

"As evidenced by the judge he managed to get to," Chase said.

Angela pointed to him. "Exactly."

"So Porter took Emmie and her mother and went on the run instead."

Zac pursed his lips as he went through the folder. "But Jordan found them—and his friends in *low* places got rid of his wife and the PI for him. And now he has his daughter back, for whatever he has in mind for her. If we want to get Emmie back legitimately, through the court system, we need irrefutable, legally obtained proof that can't be ignored."

"This flash drive was in the locked box you brought in from the PI's safe." Angela pulled up her laptop, inserted a flash drive and cast the contents onto a monitor that had been set up in the corner. A video started—two men entering a storage unit.

"Hey." Diana stiffened and sat up straighter as she watched them. One of the men had an infant held casually in his arm, not even taking care to cradle the baby's head. "That's Marty—the guy with the baby. I don't recognize the other guy, but I'm positive that's Marty."

They watched Marty approach a handsome woman in a professional-looking suit.

She carried a briefcase, which she set on the ground, then cooed over the baby for a moment, took her from Marty, turned and walked away. Marty picked up the briefcase, returned to his car and took off with his partner. The entire transaction had taken less than a minute.

And there was no doubt in Diana's mind a transaction was exactly what they'd just witnessed. Marty handed off the baby and walked away with what was probably a briefcase full of cash. "Was that what I think it was?"

Zac barely looked up from the pages he was flipping through. "According to Henry's notes, Jordan is not only involved in child trafficking, he's the *head* of an international trafficking ring."

"And," Angela added. "We're on the clock here. According to the paperwork, they never hold onto the kids for more than forty-eight hours. Tops."

No way could this be happening. The horror at what she'd just witnessed threatened to send Diana over the edge. Was this the same outcome that awaited Emmie? Would that beautiful little girl be sold to a stranger with a briefcase full of cash? And then what? What would happen to her? A soft sob escaped, despite her best efforts to contain it.

Chase closed his folder, stood and walked out.

Diana and Naomi both took off after him, leaving Zac and his agents to sort through the rest of the documents and figure out what to do.

Diana had no doubt Zac Jameson and his team were fully capable of figuring out some way of taking down Matt Jordan and his crime ring, now that they knew what was happening. Somehow, they would get Emmie back. And Zac would make sure any evidence his team gathered would be admissible in court. They didn't need her help for whatever happened next. But Chase did.

"Chase. Hey," she called after him as he strode down the hallway to the back bedroom.

He entered the room and closed the door behind him.

Diana leaned her back against the wall, frustrated. She'd give him five minutes to cool down before pounding on the door and demanding he come out and talk to her. God knew she needed a moment herself after watching that video and considering the implications.

Naomi stuffed her hands into her pockets and leaned

back against the wall across from her. "He'll be okay. It's best to just let him calm down."

Diana simply nodded, the pain clogging her throat keeping any words she might have uttered trapped there.

"Zac's team will get her back, Diana."

"Will they? Will they be able to find her before one of Jordan's thugs sells her off to the highest bidder? How could her own father do something like that? What kind of parent wouldn't do everything in the world to keep their child safe from people like that?"

Naomi's expression turned pained, and Diana instantly regretted the words that had blurted out.

Rather than respond, Naomi quirked an eyebrow and deliberately changed the subject. "So? You and Chase?"

Diana was so not ready for this conversation. She might never be. But it was better than continuing on the path she'd started down. "What do you mean?"

A slow, Cheshire cat grin spread across Naomi's face. "You know exactly what I mean. And, whenever you are ready to talk about it, I'm here for you."

"Thank you, Naomi. For being there, for understanding and for not pushing it."

"Sure thing. Just know if things work out between the two of you, I'd be thrilled for you both and happy to call you my sister."

Warmth surged through Diana. "Thank you for that. You have no idea how much it means to me. I'm sorry I'm not ready to talk. To be honest, I haven't even worked things out in my own head yet."

"I know what it's like to carry burdens, Diana. And I've seen that same pain in your eyes."

Diana wasn't sure what to say. She wanted to hug her,

tell her how sorry she was about what had happened to her husband and her little boy, but she wasn't sure if Naomi would be upset about Chase telling her.

"Chase already told you his story, and I'm assuming he told you the part I played," Naomi said before Diana could decide.

Tears pricked her lids. "I'm so sorry, Naomi. I can't even imagine the pain you must suffer every day."

"Pain, yes." She rested her head back against the wall. "But I don't blame Chase. If anyone could have kept my Connor safe, it would have been him. I know that he would have given his life to save my boy. As it was, he lost his wife…and nearly lost his own life as well. And we both know he's about to do it again."

Diana nodded. There was no sense denying it. Chase was going to go after Emmie, and there was nothing anyone could do to stop him. "But he won't be going alone."

"I didn't figure he would be." Naomi grinned and took a burner phone from her pocket, then handed it to Diana. "I can't officially be involved in what will legally be considered kidnapping, because I'm a law-enforcement official. Plus, I won't be of any help to the investigation if I'm in jail. Jameson Investigations can't officially be involved for the same reasons, though Mason discreetly put a tracking device on Emmie that Zac's not supposed to know about, since he can't afford to alienate his law-enforcement contacts."

"I understand that, and I don't expect anyone else to get involved, but I won't leave Emmie in danger, and I can't let Chase go alone, Naomi. I just can't."

"I know." She squeezed Diana's hand. "And I love you even more for it. But please don't feel like you're alone. I've gotten to understand Zac since working closely with him these past few days, and if Chase weren't going after Emmie, Mason or one of the other agents would be. Sometimes, a clandestine operation is the best we can do. But don't ever feel like you're alone. You're not. The only number programmed in there will get a burner phone on this end, and whatever resources you need will be at your disposal. Immediately, no questions asked. Just bring Emmie and Chase back safe."

"I will. I promise." Diana wrapped her arms around Naomi and hugged her tight. They both knew she might not be able to keep that promise, but she would do her absolute best not to fail.

Naomi stiffened for a second, then relaxed into her embrace and let the tears fall.

Chase tossed three sets of handcuffs into the large, black duffel bag open on the couch. He fully understood Zac had to adhere to the law, as did his agents, but there wasn't much Zac could do about a rogue agent who stormed out on his own. He checked the burner phone Mason had given him, the tracker app open and showing Emmie was still. Sleeping? He hoped so. At least then she wouldn't have to deal with whatever might be happening around her right now. And the alternative? He refused to allow the thought to take root. Diana had said Jordan wanted Emmie alive, apparently intending to sell her to the highest bidder.

A wave of nausea rose, and he forced it back down. He'd get to that child before anyone could hurt her. Of course, once Zac and his team could gather the evidence they needed to take down Jordan and his organization, Chase would have to turn her over to the authorities. And he'd be charged with kidnapping, though Zac's lawyers would argue he'd seen an immediate threat to the child and had taken precautions to shield her and keep her safe. If they had a sympathetic judge, who knew? He might even get a lenient sentence.

But none of that mattered. It seemed God was giving him a second chance, and no way would he blow it this time. He'd gladly sacrifice his life or his freedom to save that little girl.

He double-checked the bag, made sure it contained everything he'd need to rescue Emmie and then keep her out of her father's clutches until the man could be convicted for his crimes. Camping seemed like the best idea, off the grid, and no one would have to know where to find them. He could easily live off the land for months if he had to, but winter came early in the mountains. If Zac couldn't come up with something by then... He'd figure it out when the time came. He could always head south if need be.

Satisfied he was sufficiently prepared for his mission, he paused and stared at the closed door. He knew Diana would be waiting right outside. Call him a coward, but he didn't want to come face-to-face with her right now. The opportunity to see if something more existed between the two of them was the only thing he'd regret losing if he had to go on the run. But she would understand. He'd seen her risk her own life more than once to save Emmie.

He blew out a breath. She'd saved him, too. Had dragged him from that chopper with two armed gunmen nearby. As he remembered all that she'd done for him, he knew that he couldn't repay her by sneaking out the window. He'd give her a brief explanation—he owed her that much—leave out Mason's role, and by extension Zac's involvement, say goodbye, and be on his way. He braced himself and swung the door open.

Diana was leaning against the wall, tote bag over her shoulder, file folder clutched in her arms. "You done dolling yourself up in there, or what? I was beginning to think you'd never come out."

"What are you doing?" He gestured at her belongings. "Leaving?"

Why did the thought bother him so badly? It's not like he was going to hang around, either.

"Nice try, but if you think I'm not going with you, then you haven't been paying attention these past few days. I'm not letting you leave me behind." She poked him in the chest. "There is no way that's happening. So gather your things, and let's get out of here."

"Diana—"

"Forget it. You are not leaving me behind. And if you do go without me, I'll just head out on my own..." She tapped the folder she held. "To all of Jordan's known hangouts—his house, the office he uses as a front for his adoption agency, the pool hall where—"

"Okay. Stop." He shoved a hand through his hair, at a total loss as to what to do with her.

"We're partners, Chase. Isn't that what you said? And I'd like to think we're friends, too. As far as anything else between us, I can't deny my feelings for you, won't try to lie and say there's not some kind of spark between us, but I understand reality. Any opportunity we might have had to explore those feelings, to get to know each other better, went up in flames with the decision to go after Emmie. I'll even admit I'm sorry for that."

He reached out and cupped her face in his hand and

leaned in to kiss her cheek. Then he stepped back and lowered his hand to his side. "I'm sorry, too, Diana. You are an incredible woman. And I'll take you with me, but only so you don't end up getting yourself into trouble by going alone. And only on one condition."

She lifted her brow. "What's that?"

"When the time comes to hand Emmie over to the authorities, and it will come, you will turn and walk away. There's no sense both of faces charges."

"Not a chance."

"It's nonnegotiable, Diana. I can't promise you won't end up involved, but I can promise your name will never leave my lips. If you don't agree, then you don't come. Period."

"Chase, I—"

"That's the deal. Take it or leave it."

"Fine. I'll take it. Just… Let's just go." She whirled around and started toward down the hallway.

He gripped her arm and stopped her, stared deep into her eyes, trying to memorize the depth of feeling he could see whirling there. "Don't betray that trust, Diana. Please."

She turned her gaze away too soon. "I won't, Chase. No matter how much it hurts. I will never go back on my word to you."

"Fair enough." He hefted his bag over his shoulder. "Let's go."

They left out the back door while everyone else was conveniently preoccupied looking the other way, tossed their bags into a nondescript, black Subaru Outback and left the homey neighborhood behind.

Chase handed Diana the burner phone. "This is the app for the tracker Mason put on Emmie. Keep an eye on where she is. I already have the address programmed into the GPS, but let me know the second they move."

She glued her eyes to the marker that indicated Emmie's whereabouts. "Naomi knows."

"Knows what?" he asked, distracted as he pulled out of the development.

"She knows you told me about Connor."

He swallowed the lump clogging his throat, threatening to choke him.

"She doesn't blame you, you know."

Unable to speak, he simply nodded.

"She's an amazing woman."

"Yes, she is."

"She knows about us, too."

"Us?" Because he was pretty sure they'd just established that there was no *us*.

"For what it's worth…" She shifted her gaze from the phone to look at him, the streetlights washing over her. "She was happy about it, about us maybe…you know."

He smiled. He didn't know why it mattered, since they could never pursue a relationship, but somehow, knowing his sister would have approved pleased him all the same. "Thanks for that."

"You're welcome."

"And, I'm sorry. If we'd met under different circumstances…"

Diana laughed out loud, her eyes sparkling with mischief. "If we'd met under different circumstances, we would most likely have both kept our heads down, our thoughts to ourselves and passed each other with nothing more than a polite nod."

He couldn't help but laugh. She wasn't wrong.

"Seriously, though, it meant a lot to me that you felt comfortable enough to open up, to share your grief with me. It allowed me the freedom to do the same. And I really needed to." Tears shimmered in her eyes. "More than I realized. So thank you for that."

"Thank you for listening. And for not passing judgment." They fell into a companionable silence, broken only by the hum of the tires against the pavement and occasional direction from the mechanical voice of the GPS.

As he drove through the darkness, he allowed his thoughts to stray for only a moment or two, a gift to himself perhaps. He envisioned coming home at the end of the day to Diana, sitting down to dinner together, snuggling on the couch to watch a movie, working in the garden on the weekends. For just a flash, Emmie was there beside them, smiling, happy, whole.

He ruthlessly cut off the thought. That was not the life for him. His path lay elsewhere—perhaps the life of solitude he deserved. Men like him didn't get a happily ever after. Then another thought intruded. Maybe the flash of Emmie wasn't her together with him and Diana, but her superimposed over the life he'd imagined so he'd know exactly what he was giving it all up for. The end goal was for Emmie to find happiness, joy, a life filled with love. For the first time in eight years, a sense of peace settled over him, and he whispered a soft, "Thank you."

He prayed Diana would find that same contentment with her choices.

Once they exited the highway and started up the narrow New York City streets, Chase sat up straighter and leaned forward to study the neighborhood—mostly warehouses and storage buildings, a few office buildings, more long neglected brick tenements where people tended to mind their own business. At least they wouldn't have to worry about witnesses. All the better, since they might get away without Diana being seen and connected to him or Emmie. Of course, Jordan's men would recognize her, but he doubted any of them would be running down to the police station to make a statement.

Diana interrupted his thoughts. "Do you think there's a chance, if we find Emmie and she's, well…not in the best of situations, we could call the police and arrange protective custody?"

As much as he hated to dim the hope in her voice, he refused to lie to her. "Under other circumstances, probably, but this is Jordan's turf. He obviously has something to keep at least one judge under his thumb—blackmail, bribery, threats against his family, whatever. Who's to say he doesn't have others as well, or a DA, cops, politicians? It's too risky to call in the police when we don't know if they'll actually help Emmie or just tip off Jordan. The best thing we can do for Emmie is get her out of here and hide her somewhere safe while Zac works his magic. We're going to get Matt Jordan, one way or the other, but like Angela said, they never hold kids for more than forty-eight hours. If we let things run their course right now without intervening, it will probably be too late to save Emmie by the time her father is brought to justice."

She swallowed hard and turned to look out the window.

Maybe he should have tried to soften the blow, but it didn't seem to him she'd appreciate being coddled. Loved, yes. Nurtured, taken care of, adored… But that wasn't an option. Not for him.

The storage building where Emmie's tracker led them

stood at the end of the street with a highway running behind
it. Litter scattered across the parking lot, weeds overtak-
ing the narrow strip of land between it and the warehouse
next door. There were broken windows throughout, leaving
Chase wondering if they'd made a mistake, or if Jordan's
men had found the tracker, which was always a risk, and set
a trap. He kept driving, studying the layout of the building
and the property as best he could without slowing enough
to draw attention, then rounded the corner a block down.

He pulled to the side of the street in front of an indus-
trial building with smoke pouring out of the chimneys at
a cancer-inducing rate and shifted into Park. "Diana, you
don't have to do this. If I go in alone—"

"You're not doing this alone. Period." She shifted to face
him head-on, her expression determined. "Those are my
terms."

"Okay, then." He climbed out then rounded the car and
opened the hatchback. He double-checked he had everything he might need—several guns, a few knives, bolt cutters, night-vision goggles—and started to shut the door,
then thought better of it and hooked a few sets of handcuffs
to his belt. While he had a feeling none of Jordan's men
would go down without a fight, and he doubted any of them
would risk being taken alive and having to look over their
shoulders until Jordan found a way to have them shanked
in prison, you never knew. He slung the duffel bag over
his shoulder and reached up again to shut the hatchback.

Diana put a hand on his to stop him. "Don't I get a
weapon?"

He considered her pale countenance, her clenched jaw.
"I was hoping you'd wait in the car."

"Nice try."

"Fine." There wasn't time to argue. As much as he'd have preferred to bundle her off somewhere safe with an army of Zac's agents to protect her, he couldn't. He could either view her as a liability to be cared for and protected, or a partner to rely on. She'd already proven herself to be the latter. He held out a 9mm in a holster, which she clipped onto her belt, then took out a shotgun. "Do you know how to use this?"

"I do, yes."

"All right. Are you comfortable following orders?"

"Does it seem like I am?"

His first instinct was to say no, but then he thought back to the times they were in immediate danger, and he simply nodded. He didn't apologize for asking, since in this situation only one of them could lead, but he accepted she understood. "Okay, let's go get Emmie."

TEN

Diana patted her jacket pocket to be sure the phone Naomi had slipped her was still there and took comfort from the fact that someone had anticipated what they would do. At least she'd be able to sound the alarm if needed, and there would be no record of the calls. She jogged just behind Chase, careful to stick to the shadows along the building's edge as much as possible.

She wiped one hand on her pants and then the other, careful to keep the shotgun's barrel pointed away from Chase. To his credit, he never once glanced over his shoulder to check and see if she was still following him. He simply trusted that she would have his back. The thought warmed her.

She could admit she was disappointed—or devastated—that they wouldn't have the opportunity to get to know each other better. *If* they managed to survive the night and get Emmie to safety, at least one of them would be risking jail time. Who knows what would have happened had the outcome been different? Would she have had the courage to open up and let him in? Would he have been able to let go of the past enough to love her?

Love. She'd been so filled with love at one time. Could

she ever regain the ability to do so again? To love someone unconditionally? Could she open her heart to the possibility of being hurt again, risk having it shattered if he betrayed her? Perhaps she already had.

Chase lifted a hand then stopped at the end of the warehouse and peered around the corner. He lifted two fingers behind him as a signal—two men. He eased back so she could see. They were dressed all in black. Both carried very large guns as they paced back and forth along the back of the building. At least, it seemed they were probably in the right place.

Sweat slicked her hands again.

Chase gestured her to back up, then pointed to a fire escape running up one side of the building.

She nodded and slung the shotgun over her shoulder to free up her hands.

Chase holstered his weapon, then cupped his hands and boosted her up to grab the bottom rung of the ladder.

Since they couldn't risk the noise it might make to lower the ladder, she got a knee up, then scrambled over the railing and crouched down, watching the darkness for any sign of movement.

Chase jumped and easily caught the ladder, then boosted himself over the railing and landed beside her as gracefully as any large cat, as silently as any predator. He moved in front of her, then climbed the fire escape up the three stories to a window near the top of the building. He stopped and ducked on one side of the window.

Diana did the same on the opposite side. She waited for his nod, then peered into the corner of the window. The open warehouse had been turned into a storage area. Rows of storage units lined either side of metal catwalks made of grates you could see straight through to the second floor, which was the same. Great, that meant if anyone looked up, they'd easily spot Chase and Diana.

It didn't inhibit Chase, though. He removed several tools from his duffel bag, then stuck two suction cups with handles to the glass, one on each side. He gestured for her to hold the handles.

She did as instructed, while he cut through the glass around the perimeter of the window frame, then pocketed the glass cutter, took over the handles from her, eased the glass pane out and set it aside.

Diana held her breath and listened intently for the tell-tale *beep, beep, beep* of an alarm system going off. Nothing. She leaned close and whispered, "How will we know which unit she's in?"

"It'll have guards. If none have guards, we'll backtrack, cut the locks with the bolt cutter in my bag and search them all." He shouldered the bag, drew his weapon, swung one leg over the sill and ducked inside.

Diana considered the shotgun. She'd shot one before. After what happened with Liam, she'd wanted to be able to protect herself, so she'd gone to the range, learned how to shoot a shotgun and a pistol. But she'd never had to shoot at anything other than a target. The thought of having to shoot a person had bile rushing up the back of her throat. She forced it back down. The shotgun would allow her to just aim in the right direction and shoot, knowing that the pellets would spray and catch an intruder. But Emmie might be inside. Shooting like that outside was one thing. She couldn't take a chance inside the building. Instead, she kept the shotgun where it was and pulled the 9mm he'd given her, prayed for the strength to use it if she needed to, then climbed through after him.

They moved well together, as if they'd been partnered for years, as if Diana had any clue what she was doing. Still, she found it was easy to anticipate his moves. It seemed, in this situation at least, they thought alike.

They crept across the third-floor catwalk, moving quietly and methodically up and down each row, Chase's weapon trained straight ahead, Diana's aimed through the slats on the floor below them. They didn't encounter anyone. Once they'd searched every row of storage units on the third floor, all of which stood open, they descended a stairway in the far corner of the building and began to systematically search the second floor.

Unlike the third floor, these units were all closed and padlocked. No way could they break into all of them as they worked their way down. They'd better come across some indication of where Emmie was being kept soon, because if they had to return to the second floor and cut locks off literally hundreds of units and search each one, they were going to need backup. Or about a week. The thought that any or all of those units might have children hidden inside them sent a chill up her spine.

Chase held up his hand for her to stop and tilted his head.

A man's voice drifted to them.

Pressing her back against the wall beside Chase, praying no one looked up through the grated floor, she cocked her head and strained to hear what the guy was saying.

"...on his way to pick her up."

The rest of what he said was too muffled for her to make out.

Apparently, Chase agreed, as he crept toward the direction the voice came from.

Two rows over, they found what they were looking for. Through the catwalk's grates, Diana spotted two men, one of them unlocking the second storage unit from the end, the other with his back to the wall between the garage-style door and the unit, gun raised, keeping watch.

"Cover me," Chase whispered and took off.

Diana froze. She scanned every inch of the floor below them. The guy with the keys tucked them in his jacket pocket, bent and unhooked the padlock, then rolled up the door. When he looked around before disappearing inside the unit, she recognized him as Marty from the woods. While Marty entered the unit, the other guy held his position.

And then Chase was there. He emerged from the shadows, landed a solid blow to the guard's temple, then guided him silently to the ground out of sight of the door. Once he rolled him over and cuffed him, Chase slid the weapon aside, then patted the guy down and stood alongside the door.

When Marty emerged carrying a small child—her long, blond hair covering her face, her body limp in his arms—Chase caught him from behind and pressed the gun against the back of his head. "Put the girl down. Gently. Now."

The man glanced at his partner unconscious and cuffed on the floor, then did as instructed. He lowered the girl, who couldn't be more than a year old, to the cold, metal floor.

She didn't even flinch.

Diana had to get to her, but she didn't dare leave Chase without backup before he secured Marty.

She crouched lower, concentrating on the child, searching for any sign of life. Had she just seen her chest move? She wasn't sure. Keeping one eye on Chase as he cuffed the guy, she held her breath and waited for the movement to be repeated.

Something cold and hard jammed against the back of her head. "Don't move."

She froze, then lifted her hands slowly, even as she was kicking herself for making such a stupid mistake. She'd been so caught up with watching Chase and the child, she'd missed someone coming up behind her. Some lookout she'd turned out to be.

He took the gun from her hand, then lifted the shotgun sling off her shoulder and braced the weapon against a door. He shoved her face-first against the wall and searched her for weapons, then yanked her back by the hair. "Do not make a sound. Do not alert him in any way, or I will shoot him from here before he can even glance in your direction. Got it?"

She nodded against the pressure he maintained on the handful of hair, tears leaking from the corners of her eyes.

"Walk, now. Quietly."

She did exactly as he said, walking straight ahead, then turned in the direction he indicated when they reached the end of the row. She followed his directions down the stairs. By that point, he no longer needed to guide her. She knew exactly where he wanted her to go.

When she rounded the corner, Marty and the other guy were cuffed, and Chase was bent over the child, feeling for a pulse in her neck. Leading with the gun, he surged to his feet.

"I wouldn't, if I were you." The guy yanked Diana's

hair harder, pulling her closer in front of him, using her as a human shield.

Chase froze, weapon aimed at the guy's head. Or at least, it would have been if Diana wasn't in the way. "Drop it, Jordan. It's over."

Jordan? She was being held by Emmie's father? Since he'd come up behind her, she hadn't gotten a look at his face.

She spared a glance at the little girl. She was too pale, breathing shallow, lips tinged blue. Drugged? Possibly. Either way, she needed medical attention as soon as possible. It wasn't Emmie, but it was still a child in need of help.

Fear poured through her, and she began to shake. If this wasn't Emmie, then where was she? She had to be here somewhere. And they needed to get to her. She might be in the same condition as this little girl. Determination replaced some of the fear. They would find Emmie. Any other outcome was unacceptable. But how?

Jordan had them at gunpoint, and they still didn't know which storage unit held Emmie.

While the guy's attention was riveted on Chase, Diana slid a hand slowly into her jacket pocket. She ran her thumb over the burner phone's screen, tapped the bottom corner where the phone icon should be, where the only number stored was on speed dial, and pressed what she hoped was Send, praying she'd managed to summon help.

Diana's gaze met Chase's and held as she tried to convey all of her regret that things between them would end this way, that she'd failed him when he'd trusted her, then she mouthed, *Shoot him.*

Chase ignored her. "Drop it, man."

"I'm going to count to three, then you either put down

your gun or she dies," Jordan said, his voice calm and confident.

"Listen, man." Chase's voice held steady, too. "The first thing I'm going to do once you let her go is care for that child, which will give you a chance to flee."

He shifted Diana tighter against him. "One."

Chase's weapon didn't falter. "If you turn and run now, you might get away."

"Two."

Diana held her breath, kept her gaze glued to Chase so she wouldn't miss even the most subtle direction. Tremors coursed through her.

Chase inched closer to the little girl, which also brought him a step closer to Jordan.

"Thr—"

Diana whirled toward his gun hand, grabbed his wrist in a desperate two-handed grip.

Chase fired, catching Jordan in the shoulder, forcing him to release his hold on her hair.

She staggered out of the way, trying to give Chase a clear shot.

Two gunshots went off in rapid succession, almost simultaneously.

Pain tore through Diana's collarbone, spread across her chest, and then she went blessedly numb. As she started to fall, darkness encroached, tunneling her vision until only Chase remained. She tried to smile, tried to tell him it was okay. Then her head hit the metal flooring, and everything went black.

"No!" Chase screamed. *No, no, no.*

Diana lay in a pool of blood, the little girl limp and unresponsive between them. The past crept in to overlay the present—he saw Victoria down, Connor on the ground, Chase lying there, desperately trying to reach them, unable to move. The world slowed until everything around him remained perfectly still, as if the world was waiting for him to fail once more, as he had the last time. Fear paralyzed him. This couldn't happen again. *Please, God, not again.*

No way. Not this time. He searched for calm, prayed for clarity. This was not eight years ago. It was not his wife lying there, or his nephew, and he was not helpless. And now, unlike the past, the bad guy lay dead, no longer a threat.

Chase dove toward Diana, dropped to his knees and felt for a pulse even as he whipped out his phone, called Zac and set the phone down on speaker.

"Jameson."

"She's hit. Diana's hit." He sucked in a breath, the cool air burning his lungs, as he wrapped his arms around her and cradled her close, staring down at her too-pale face.

"We're almost there."

"Almost here?" That didn't make sense. The entire situation was surreal, as if time was surging forward, and he was struggling to catch up. He had to get his head out of the past, deal with the present. Diana was injured, the little girl was unconscious and Emmie was still missing. He'd have time to put all the pieces together and fall apart later. For now... "But how? Why?"

"We were nearby when Diana's call came in. It's a little muffled, but we were able to make out and record the entire conversation."

"She called? What were you doing here?"

"Oh, please, Chase. Naomi, Mason and I were on a chopper minutes after you pulled away from the curb. I might not have been able to sanction the operation, but you didn't really think I'd let you go in without backup, did you?"

He'd known he'd have help if he called, but he didn't expect all of them, his sister included, to put their reputations on the line. "Plausible deniability."

"Exactly. If you were picked up, you could honestly say you'd gone in alone. At least, to the best of your knowledge."

"I don't know what to say, Zac. Thank you."

"Thank me later. Right now, where are Jordan and his men?"

He was going to have to lay Diana down, leave her to check the girl. He held her closer, his tears dripping into her hair, and whispered an apology.

"Jordan's dead." Chase's shot had found its target, had taken him out instantly, but not in time to save Diana from being shot. "One of his guys is unconscious and cuffed, the other is cuffed, but he took off in the confusion. I couldn't leave Diana and the little girl to go after him."

"You've got Emmie?"

"What?" Then he realized Zac would not have been privy to that knowledge. As his head started to clear, training took over. "Listen, Zac. Diana is bleeding but stable. I have an unconscious female child about a year old. I need the police, an ambulance and a search team. Emmie has to be in one of these storage units, but we haven't found her yet."

"ETA is about three minutes for the first responders."

"All right. Got it." He reached to end the call, then stopped. "And, Zac."

"Yeah?"

"Thanks, man."

Static crackled over the line. "Anytime, Chase. But there is one thing."

"What's that?"

"I'm revoking your vacation privileges. No more time off for you."

He managed a smile. "I can't argue with that."

He disconnected the call. "Diana."

No response.

"Hey." He tapped her cheek. He didn't know for sure why she'd passed out. Pain from the bullet wound, maybe? She'd gone down so quickly, before blood loss would have rendered her unconscious, but she had hit her head when she'd landed. "Diana. Wake up."

She stirred.

Oh, thank You, God. "Come on, Diana. You've got to wake up now."

Her eyes shot open, and she started to lurch upright, then groaned and pressed a hand to her collarbone. Her eyes rolled up and started to flutter closed again.

"Hey." He shifted her away from him and lowered her gently to the floor. No matter how badly he wanted to hold her, assure himself she would pull through, he needed to get the first-aid kit from his bag from where he'd left it around the corner, and there were still at least two children in danger—the little girl and Emmie. "Listen to me. You have to wake up. You've been injured, and I need you to wake up now."

"Emmie?"

He cringed as he stood, then bent over the little girl and felt for a pulse. "We don't have her yet. We have to find her, but I can't do anything until I know you're awake and alert."

That seemed to clear some of the cobwebs. She opened her eyes and turned her head toward him. "The other little girl...is she okay? Where did Marty and his partner go?"

"Her pulse is strong, and she's breathing. Is Marty the guy cuffed over there? Or is he the one who got away?"

Diana turned her head slowly, then frowned. "That's not Marty. It's the other guy."

Chase scooped the little girl up and brought her to Diana. "If I help you sit up against the wall, can you stay awake and keep an eye on her?"

"Yeah." She tried to scoot back, and he hooked her beneath the arm and helped her. Once she was situated, he lowered the child into her arm on her uninjured side. "Where are your weapons?"

"Um..." She closed her eyes, and he wanted nothing more than to hold her and reassure her she was safe. But she wasn't. Not until he knew where Marty had disappeared to. If Marty was smart, he'd be halfway out of the country by now, but the guy didn't strike Chase as a genius. "Jordan took the handgun and left the shotgun upstairs."

"All right. Stay put." He handed her his gun, wrapped her fingers around the grip. "Zac is on his way with backup, but if you see Marty, take him down. You understand me?"

"Yeah. Yeah. I got it." She hugged the girl closer against her and shifted the weapon onto her lap past the child.

Not ideal, but it was the best he could do for right now. He jogged to where he'd left his bag, looking up through the grates, searching the second floor for any sign of movement. Nothing.

Sirens wailed in the distance.

Chase grabbed the duffel bag and hurried back to Diana, then dropped it on the floor beside her and opened it. He pulled out the first-aid kit, grabbed a gauze pad and pressed it against a wound on her head where she must have hit the floor when she fell. He wound a bandage around her head to hold the gauze in place. Then he checked the bullet wound in her collarbone. He tipped her chin up so he could look into her eyes. She'd lost a lot of blood already and appeared to be in shock. "You doing okay?"

She winced against the pain when she shifted to look past him. "I'm sorry."

"Sorry?" He scanned the area—still clear. The sirens sounded like they were right outside the building. "Sorry for what?"

"I was trying to look through the grates in the floor to see if the little girl was breathing, and I didn't hear Jordan come up behind me." Her breathing hitched and she stifled a small sob.

"Hey. Listen to me." He cradled both her cheeks in his hands, swiped a tear away with his thumb. "You have nothing to be sorry for. It wasn't your fault. I'm just glad you're going to be okay. Is there anything you need?"

Tears streamed down her cheeks. "Right now, I just need you to find Emmie. Please."

He studied her another second, kissed the top of her head and released her.

He grabbed the bolt cutter from his bag and started with the storage unit beside the one Marty had taken the girl from. He cut through the padlock, yanked it off and tossed it aside, then rolled up the door.

The first thing to hit him was the stench, and he gagged. A dirty mattress lay in one corner. But, other than that, the unit was empty. His entire body vibrated with rage. Had another child been kept there? Where was he or she now? He had to move, had to concentrate on the children he could still save. There would be time later to try to re-cover some of the others Jordan had taken. He'd dedicate his life to the search. He turned away, grabbed the cutters and almost ran smack into Marty standing in the doorway, hands still cuffed but in front of him now. He lifted the gun he was holding toward Chase.

A gunshot hit Marty's arm, and he whirled toward the shooter. The second shot took him in the shoulder and forced him back against the doorjamb.

Chase wrestled the gun from his hand, and shoved him face-first onto the floor. He didn't dare glance over his shoulder into the horrid storage unit, or he might lose his battle with control. "Move again, and I'll stop you perma-nently. Do you understand me?"

Marty nodded as he gripped his shoulder and moaned.

Chase looked in the direction the shots had come from and found Diana, shoulder leaning against the wall, one arm hanging limp at her side, weapon still trained on Marty. Pain or blood loss had leeched all the color from her face, dark, nearly black, circles ringed her eyes and her hand trembled, but still she stood strong and offered a shaky smile. "I thought you could use a hand."

"You were right." He grinned and shook his head. "But I thought you said you weren't that good a shot?"

She held his gaze. "I'm not. Usually."

The little girl lay against the wall a few feet away where Diana had been sitting with her.

"She's still unconscious?"

"Yes."

"All right. Why don't you sit down there before you pass out again?"

She turned so her back leaned against the wall, then bent her knees and slid down to sit. She braced the gun atop her knees. "Finish searching. I'll cover you until someone better shows up."

He grinned. "There is no one better."

"Ditto."

At a loss for words, he nodded and started toward the unit on the other side of the open one, then paused and turned back to her. "For the record, there's no one I'd rather have backing me up than you."

This time, when he rolled up the door, he found a little girl of about three unconscious on a sleeping bag in the middle of the room, her long brown curls tangled around her face and neck. He ran to her, checked her pulse, her respiration—all good, but she was out cold. He resisted the urge to bundle her up and take her out of there. It was better to leave her where she was until medics arrived. He wouldn't have even moved the other girl if she hadn't been lying in the open.

The sound of a door crashing open beneath a battering ram brought a wave of relief. "Police!"

He stepped out of the unit. "We're over here."

Footsteps pounded through the building, and then Zac was there, weapon drawn. "Everything okay?"

Chase gestured toward the open storage unit door behind him, then stepped aside.

Zac took one glimpse inside, looked around at all the other units in sight, on this floor and up through the grates at the second and third floors, then walked away without another word, pulling out his phone as he rounded the corner.

Chaos ensued as police officers lined the rows, rescue workers cut locks off storage units, and EMTs rushed in wherever they found children. As time passed, Chase started to grow anxious. They still hadn't found Emmie, and with Jordan dead, they couldn't even bargain with him for her release.

They'd found six children, along with evidence that three other units had once been occupied, by the time the EMTs loaded Diana onto a stretcher.

Chase set aside his bolt cutters and ran to her. He gripped her hand. "Are you starting to feel any better?"

She nodded and squeezed his hand tight. "Have you found her?"

"Not yet." But he wouldn't give up until he did.

"What if—"

"Hey. I won't believe that." Careful of the IV line the EMTs had started, he hugged her, kissed the top of her head, then stepped back. "I'm sorry I can't go with you to the hospital. I can't leave until—"

"Hey. I'll be fine. Besides, if you left this place without searching every last inch of it for Emmie and rescuing whatever children were being held here, you wouldn't be the man I lo—" She looked up at him, injured, vulnerable, her eyes wide but crystal clear, and took a deep breath. "You wouldn't be the man I fell in love with."

He closed his eyes, just for one moment, then opened them and pulled her into his arms, cocooning her in his embrace. He nuzzled close to her ear and whispered, "I love you, too, Diana. I never thought I'd be capable of loving anyone again, but you managed to sneak past my defenses and wriggle your way straight into my heart."

She sobbed against him, clinging tightly.

He relished the feel of her in his arms, the scent of orange blossoms, the steady beat of a heart filled with more love than he'd ever have thought possible. "I promise you I'll be at the hospital as soon as we're done here."

"Thank you."

He hugged her tighter, wishing time would stop and give him one minute to just enjoy feeling again. He stepped back, before he wouldn't be able to.

"Chase!" Zac waved to him from the front door.

"I gotta go." He turned and ran back toward the building, turning to look back once and wave as the paramedics loaded Diana into the ambulance.

Zac moved aside, making way for Naomi to run through the door, sobbing, Emmie clutched in her arms.

Chase ran to meet her. "Is she okay? Is she hurt?"

Emmie lifted her head from Naomi's shoulder, spotted Chase and reached out to him.

He looked her over as best he could while Naomi shifted her into his arms, took stock that she seemed awake, but sleepy, and unharmed. Then, losing his battle for control, he dropped to his knees with her in his arms and cried. "Oh, God, thank You for saving them both."

Naomi knelt across from him, pressed her forehead against his, hugged him. "She's okay, Chase. They're both going to be okay."

He nodded, struggling for control of emotions he had no hope of regaining, and wrapped his arms around Naomi, hugging Emmie between them.

Emmie clung to him, crying, and buried her head against his chest.

"I have to tell Diana." He sniffed.

Naomi hugged him once more then stood and held out

a hand to help him to his feet. "Zac held the ambulance, they're waiting for you."

He nodded. "Are you all right, Naomi?"

She sniffed and wiped the tears from her cheeks. "I am, Chase. For the first time in eight years, I really am okay. Now go. Angela is going to drive me to the hospital. She'll follow behind you, and we'll meet you guys there."

"Okay." He held Emmie tighter against him. "Thank you, Naomi."

"You're welcome."

He jogged across the street to where the ambulance sat, a paramedic standing beside the door waiting for him. When Chase reached them, the guy swung the back door open, and Chase climbed inside with Emmie in his arms.

Diana turned toward the sound and opened her eyes, then burst into tears. "You found her!"

Emmie lifted her head at the sound of Diana's voice. A huge grin spread across her face, and she dove into Diana's outstretched arms.

Chase sat beside the stretcher and shifted until he could embrace them both, and held them close. He might just never let them go.

EPILOGUE

Emmie leaned her head against Diana's shoulder and popped her thumb into her mouth. Therapy with Maddy had helped her tremendously this past year. She rarely woke screaming in the night any longer. She'd started preschool two mornings a week to help her meet and interact with other children before she'd begin kindergarten next year. But she still hadn't broken the thumb-sucking habit when stressed. And sitting outside the courthouse, waiting for Chase to return, definitely counted as stress. But it was better than being inside. At least, for Emmie.

Diana ran a hand over Emmie's hair, enjoying the smooth, soft feel, as she gazed out over the mountains reflected on the placid surface of the lake. The autumn leaves painted a colorful canvas. A cool breeze ruffled her hair, and she tilted her face up toward the still-warm sun. Winter would come to the mountains soon enough, and she and Chase would snuggle before the fireplace in the cabin he'd moved into with her after they'd been married in June. Naomi had stood as her maid of honor, and Zac had been Chase's best man. They'd had a small wedding, filled with love and joy. And Emmie had stood between them, all smiles. Diana had received temporary custody of her, thanks to Maddy's and Zac's intervention, on the night Emmie's father had been killed, and the two of them had been together, and inseparable, ever since.

But today... Well, today was the day they'd find out if the adoption would go through. If all went well inside, she and Chase would become Emmie's parents legally and permanently. She'd prayed long and hard these past months, and she couldn't repress a thread of fear. Not that there was any reason the adoption should be denied, but Diana couldn't help but worry.

She shifted on the bench. Her collarbone was still occasionally achy, but it didn't matter. Having Emmie close to her was all that mattered.

Chase's hands landed on her shoulders from behind her, the warmth seeping through her lightweight jacket as he squeezed and leaned over to kiss her head. "It's done."

Instead of asking, she simply hugged Emmie closer and let the tears fall as she continued to watch the lake, searching for peace and calm.

Chase rounded the bench and sat down close enough for their legs to touch. Emmie scooted over until she sat half on his lap and half on Diana's. Sitting between them like that, she completed them.

Chase hugged Emmie with one arm and wrapped the other around Diana's shoulders, pulling her close to round out the little circle of she saw as their family, no matter what the court might have decided. "She's ours, Diana."

A sob tore free, and she buried her face in Emmie's hair and cried.

Emmie turned and wrapped her arms around both their necks, then squeezed with all her might. "I love you, Mama. I love you, Papa."

"We love you, too, baby girl." Chase's voice was raspy with emotion.

She'd taken to calling them Mama and Papa a few months ago, when she seemingly decided she wanted to stay with them no matter the judge's decision—different from the Mommy she'd loved and lost and the Daddy she'd feared.

Naomi approached with Zac and a mile-wide grin. The two of them had taken to spending a lot of time together, though she'd refused his offer to go to work for Jameson Investigations, saying she wasn't quite ready to leave the small town of Shady Creek just yet. But he'd left the invitation open for her. "Congratulations."

Diana nodded, still unable to find her voice.

Chase stood and hugged his sister.

Zac clapped Chase on the back.

"I don't know how I can ever thank you. For everything, Zac. Things might have ended much differently without your help. I don't know how I can ever repay you."

"That's okay, I do." His gaze fell on Diana, and he cleared his throat.

Naomi reached a hand out to Emmie. "Mind if I take this little one right over there for ice cream?"

Diana stiffened, then worked to relax as she looked toward the small ice-cream parlor across the street that Naomi had pointed out, in plain view of not only Diana, but also Chase and Zac. "Of course."

"Great." She held Emmie's hand and waved, then called over her shoulder, "We'll bring you all back something."

"Sit." Zac gestured toward the bench where they'd been sitting, then stuffed his hands in his pockets and rocked back on his heels. "You don't have to answer today, Diana, or even tomorrow, but I'd like you to consider coming to work for me."

She opened her mouth to protest, tell him her days would be filled with caring for Emmie for now, and that when she was ready to work full-time again, she was eager to return to the Shady Creek Fire Department.

But he held up a hand to stop her. "Not on a full-time basis, but now and then when we need you, for cases where I think you could help, like Shae Payne does."

She remembered meeting Shae for the first time, feeling comforted by her presence, by the knowledge that she'd survived what Diana had been going through. If she could do that for someone else, how could she refuse? "Yes. You can call me if you need me."

He grinned. "I'll do that."

"In the meantime," Chase said and turned to face her. "Let us tell you what Zac has found out before Naomi returns with Emmie."

"Marty received a life sentence for his role in kidnapping the sixteen children that were found in that warehouse." Diana felt the familiar burn of outrage when she thought of all the children those vicious men had harmed. There was some relief in knowing that all of the children had been reunited with their parents and were doing as well as could be expected, but they never should have been harmed in the first place. Zac continued, "Marty carried on to anyone who would listen about Jordan not just killing Emmie like he'd told him to. Said Jordan got greedy, decided why should he just put a hit out on her when she could net them an extra few million. That didn't earn him any points with the prosecutor, who refused to offer any kind of plea deal."

"Did you find out why Jordan killed Emmie's mother and Henry Porter?"

"It was what we expected—Emmie's mother knew Jordan was up to something illegal, had seen him with one of the little girls one time, and hired Porter to find out what was going on. Porter got a little too close, and Jordan took them both out."

"What about the kids we were too late to save?" Those were the ones that kept her up at night. She slid her hand into Chase's.

"The police found some records when they searched the building and a few more when they tossed Jordan's residence and office, and we've been able to recover several of the children who were taken. We're working to find all of them, Diana. And I promise you I won't stop trying until we bring every last one of them home."

She nodded.

"And we did manage to take down a major trafficking ring. Not only did we get Marty and most of Jordan's muscle, but we also got a couple of lawyers, a bogus adoption agency and what they referred to as a baby broker."

She'd have to hold on to that in the wee hours of the morning when she wept for the children yet to be found. And with that, her decision was confirmed. When Zac did finally reach out and ask her to come, she'd ask Naomi to stay with Emmie and catch the first flight out, no doubt a private one Zac chartered. She smiled, suddenly feeling much lighter. They might not have won the entire war, but they'd had a few major victories that were well worth celebrating with her new family.

"Oh, and just so you know, we were able to find out who leaked your whereabouts the night at the cabin."

She held her breath, hoping it hadn't been someone from the fire department.

"It was one of Naomi's deputies. One of Jordan's guys got to him, threatened to take out his family, so he talked."

She lowered her gaze and nodded. "What's going to happen to him?"

Zac shrugged. "Naomi's a very understanding woman, but I honestly don't know."

Emmie danced back across the street, holding tightly to Naomi's hand. When they reached the side where Diana and Chase stood waiting for her, she let go and charged them.

Naomi laughed and held up a white bag. "There's a picnic table down by the lake. Why don't we all go celebrate with ice cream?"

Emmie hooked Diana's and Chase's hands and started running toward the shore, then yelled, "One, two, three jump," and launched herself into the air between them.

They swung her high, her laughter echoing across the lake, making the day just about perfect.

* * * * *

If you enjoyed
Hiding The Witness,
be sure to check out more gripping stories
by Deena Alexander!

Discover more at LoveInspired.com

Dear Reader,

Thank you so much for sharing Chase and Diana's story! I love flawed characters, whose internal conflicts are as unique and challenging as the danger they find themselves in.

One of the things both Chase and Diana struggle with is the ability to trust. They've both endured tragedies in the past and are having a difficult time learning to trust themselves and others again. I think all of us go through trials in our lives that make it difficult to open up and trust one another, but as long as we continue to trust in God, I believe we can learn to trust others again.

I hope you've enjoyed sharing Chase and Diana's journey as much as I enjoyed creating it. If you'd like to keep up with my new stories, you can find me on Facebook, www.facebook.com/DeenaAlexanderAuthor, and Twitter, twitter.com/DeenaAlexanderA. Or sign up for my newsletter, gmail.us10.list-manage.com/subscribe?u=d7e6e9ec dc0888d7324788ffc&id=42d52965df

Deena Alexander

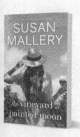   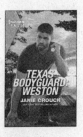